BLAZE THE GRID

A NOVEL BY

KEVIN FLANDERS

KEVIN FLANDERS

Blaze the Grid – Copyright © May 2018 by Kevin Flanders

All rights reserved.

This is a work of fiction. All characters, locations, ideas, and related content were either invented by the author or presented fictitiously. Additionally, all organizations, businesses, associations, and other entities featured in this work were presented in a fictitious context.

Excluding reviews, the accounts of this work may not be reproduced, sold, uploaded, disseminated, stored in a retrieval system, or displayed in any form without the written consent of the author.

BLAZE THE GRID

ACKNOWLEDGEMENTS

The *Gridlocked* series continues to blaze along thanks to the tireless help of the following friends and family:

Jeremy Bedson
Mike Flanders
Susana Flanders
Dominick Palmucci
Kimmy Palmucci

ALSO FROM KEVIN FLANDERS

Please check out the following novels:

WELCOME TO HARROW HALL

INSIDE THE ORANGE GLOW

LASER TAG

THE INHABITANTS (trilogy)

THE GRID AWAKENS (third book in the *Gridlocked* series)

BURN, DO NOT READ!

For more information about upcoming works, visit www.kmflanders.wordpress.com.

BLAZE THE GRID

For Lucky, my friend and protector for eleven unforgettable years. Like pawprints in the snow, you imprinted your many quirks and rituals in our lives and never stopped smiling. You overcame so much and asked for so little. You showed us the fine arts of hunting for moles and eating off foreheads. You were always there for us.

Rest in Peace, Lucky Bus.

KEVIN FLANDERS

Chapter 1

Social media squabbles had made their incessant eruptions that day.

Pigskin pundits had prognosticated Sunday's scores.

And a homeless Army veteran had shot himself to death outside an Omaha bar, forgotten no longer.

Indeed, it had been a typical day in the nation, but now, in the night...

...At Tantasqua High School in Sturbridge, Massachusetts, Randy Wilner came trundling and clattering awake with all the grace of a car limping into the breakdown lane with a flat. He rolled into a bank of lockers, his left arm shooting not merely with pain but fireworks of agony. It had been broken, he knew it absolutely, same for his nose, which clicked and leaked like a troubled faucet. It had been twisted by the bastard's sucker punch, Randy not wanting to shoot him, not wanting to kill anyone, just trying to bring him and the others under control.

Even during his fragile, pained sleep there had been dreams. Randy had initially dreamt of his family and his fellow officers at the Brimfield Police Department, but then his dreams had taken a strange route, bringing him back to Brimfield Elementary School, where he visited children on Community Reading Day every year. Except in the dream which quickly became a nightmare, he'd explained to the frightened little faces, tears in his eyes, that he couldn't keep them and their families safe anymore.

BLAZE THE GRID

The grid is down, kids. The grid is down. The school buses aren't coming to bring you home today. Your parents aren't coming to pick you up. You're on your own – we're all on our own. Run and hide, kids! They're coming! He's coming!

***

The wind arrived like a whispering phantom through the cracked window of Harry Freed's bedroom, something not quite right about it.

For just a moment, barely back from sleep, reflexively reaching for his wife's shoulder, Harry ascended to the zenith of fear, a nightmare having brought him there. It was one of those nightmares that, in its throes, the sleeping mind is assailed by an ancient terror, the heart's locked doors and scars of memory opened helplessly, a dark thing creeping in.

Coming fully awake now, realizing that his wife wasn't there and would never again lie beside him, the heavy oak doors of the heart shut and locked again, Harry's nightmare of course seemed inane. He'd gone to a world in which teenagers led the government, passing laws with bombastic and incorrectly spelled words, communicating not through speech but social media, imprisoning and executing people with a shrug and a whim. It was a world where people rarely looked up from devices at dinner, where creativity was all but lost, journalists no longer reporting the news but instead covering what the government told them to cover. The elderly were locked away like the medieval mentally ill, infants handed a bottle and a shifter, the sky itself turned into a bloody glowing screen, the stars its keys. It was a society driven by decadence, tunnelized, the world burrowing deeper and deeper underground, the SR1 and SR2000 and subterranean maglevs putting airlines out of business, fast and faster and fastest, marriages surprisingly still performed with vows while arbitrators waited at honeymoon suites, parents replaced by guardians, books supplanted and forgotten.

Suddenly the society in Harry's nightmare didn't seem all that distant. You could already make love in the SR dark, or jam sesh on your way to the concert. You could have your rental car pick you up at any location and, once your trip was over, you grabbed your things and let the car drop itself off at the lot. You could take Transrapid maglevs with corny subdivision names that sounded vaguely like the community newspapers that had once thrived – the Atlantic Arrow, the Sunbelt Sonic, the Capitol Clipper, the Desert Dasher, the Northwest Navigator, the Pacific Pacer – and you would reach your destination before the robot poured your next cup of coffee, though not nearly as rapidly as the vactrains might one day go, when Harry's nightmare world reached abject fruition.

Fast, faster, fastest, yet there was something to be said for slowing down and watching a sunrise. How much was everybody missing while infected with the need for speed?

Harry shuddered, took a drink of water, glad to be thirsty again, gladder still to be free of the nightmare. His sickness – the reason for his excessive sleep – had been a fairly bad one, but like a stubborn writer's block it was running its course and he was coming back around again, the cool night wind invigorating...but wrong.

Tinged with smoke.

Harry felt gooseflesh rising, not just because of the smell but the darkness. Too dark. The hallway light, which he always left on, had clicked off somewhere between Harry's slippage into sleep around eleven and now.

The alarm clock's green glow was absent as well, the room as dark as a grave. Achingly, Harry creaked up into a sitting position and rested against the backboard, his eyes adjusting to the no longer perfect darkness of a power outage. The room was gently flickering, tinted orange.

Vestiges from his nightmare lingering – *Lord, those kids were frightening* – Harry kicked into his slippers and padded over to the side window, which gave him a look at the northern woods that often found him hiking. The little pleasures were important now that Janey was gone, sweet, beautiful Janey, whom he'd met back when they were both Londoners, the U.S. a foreign land full of opportunities. Fenway Park, which would eventually become their summertime sanctuary, was as obscure as the rest of the west.

Janey. She'd been taken too soon, the world so much colder in her absence, nothing the same, and how could it ever be the same again after more than forty years together?

Harry was staring wide-eyed into the woods, transfixed by small pockets of orange glaring out of the darkness like demonic eyes. The fires, little more than torches at this distance, were burgeoning at the nearest houses – the DiMarteer and Perron residences – which were less than a quarter of a mile through the woods.

"My God," Harry rasped, and it took him a few stunned moments to find his legs.

Bumbling about the darkness, he knocked the lamp off his nightstand and flung open the drawer, grabbing the flashlight Janey had always insisted on keeping there. It had come in handy a time or two, and by its trusty light Harry made his way to the dresser and threw a sweatshirt and pants over his pajamas.

What the hell is going on? It must be arson!

An opponent of cell phones and E-books and the latest unveiling, shifters, Harry's only hope of communication was the landline…which was dead.

Feeling a little dizzy, as though he'd just stepped off a carnival ride, his stomach mildly nauseous – certainly not septic, as the students in Harry's high school English class would say – he hurried downstairs to the front door and through it. On the porch with his flashlight, he took in a heavier smell of smoke, guided in by a breeze.

In a matter of minutes the fires had expanded rapidly. A collection of sounds drifted sinuously through the woods, some with greater clarity than others. One of those sounds was a faint scream amid the roaring fires.

Staring through the woods, mesmerized helplessly by the orange beacons, Harry glimpsed something large scuttling through the trees, perhaps twenty feet in. It moved with quick, heavy steps that kicked up the recently fallen leaves; then it abruptly stopped, waited in the darkness, seemingly aware of Harry's presence.

A deer? A bear? The arsonist?

Harry didn't stick around for a closer examination, rushing inside to grab his 12-gauge shotgun. A glance at the wall clock told him it was half past one in the morning, but it seemed as if only minutes had passed since he'd been reading almost vacuously around eleven in the grip of exhaustion and sickness, the paragraphs of his Dean Koontz novel going blurry.

He would never finish the book.

"You better get off my property before I blow your damn head off!" Harry shouted after returning to the porch. He thought he could see the intruder's shifting form in the dark woods – a little deeper now. His flashlight didn't make it nearly that far out, though, and searching for features was like trying to discern an object just below the ocean's surface.

"Cops are on their way!" Harry added, scanning for further movement in the windswept woods, his stomach beginning to sour again.

Christ, get in the car! People could be trapped in those houses. Where's the fire department?

It occurred then to Harry, and not without a shiver, that he hadn't heard any sirens or blasting horns. Even with everyone squared firmly up on the grid, emergency vehicles still featured sirens and flashing lights, just in case they came across a grid dodger.

Harry jogged over to his Pontiac and set the gun in the back seat. But when he tried to call up the grid, there was nothing but a blank screen on the Q. Where the hell was the damn lady's voice asking him for information, the bloody computer lass who would plug him into the system and tell him for the umpteenth time that there were no defects?

Slapping the screen with frustration, Harry glanced through the windshield and glimpsed something briefly emerge from the woods and then recede, so quickly it made him lurch back and wonder if he'd seen it at all, like a dorsal fin breaking the water at twilight. One second it was there, and the next…

"What the hell is going on?"

Harry tried the Q again, but there were seemingly no tricks left in the magic screen, only futile darkness, Harry's dystopian nightmare future at its inception.

It's all connected – the power outage, the fires, the grid going down!

Harry cranked open the door and vomited, managing only a few dribbles of bile that fell in skeins to the gravel. When he looked up again, full of dark expectation, there was nothing within or beyond the woods but blazes of brilliant orange.

Gathering his wallet, a half-empty bottle of water from the cup holder, and his Remington from the back seat, Harry took off unsteadily into the woods, desperate to save whoever needed saving, clueless as to how the hell he'd do it.

With every step, the wind and its most prominent passenger – ravenous smoke – seemed to strengthen.

**

Gene and the other kids were growing restless, spurred by the hot coals of fear and uncertainty that rattled around their hearts.

Where were the adults?

Rock and Mikaela had both said they'd be back. That had been a long time ago. *Stay here*, Rock had urged. *No matter what, don't leave this room.*

But what if the man came instead – the man who'd said he would find Gene anywhere, the man who'd hurt him, the man who could fly?

Gene brought a hand delicately to his bandaged forehead, pain springing up from beneath. There were twelve other kids in the room, a few of them gathered at the door, their faces pressed up against the windowed rectangle. A while ago two older kids had moved the babies to other classrooms, and now the room was much quieter...and somehow scarier. Cots were spread out as if a massive indoor campout would take place, except this definitely wouldn't be like the Boy Scout event Gene had attended last year, with snacks and stories and friends. He didn't know any of these kids, and there would be no campfire and marshmallows tonight, only scared faces and tears.

Gene wished those kids would get away from the door. If the man came searching down the hall, sneaky like the wind, peering into every classroom with shifting eyes sunken beneath a tattered hood, you didn't want to be standing at the door!

"We should hide," Gene told the girl sitting next to him. He pointed to the student desks that had been heaped against the walls to make room for the cots. "We can hide behind those."

"Okay." Her voice was tiny, the voice of a ballerina on a jewelry box. Her face was streaked red from crying.

Gene didn't know her name. He hadn't thought to ask, too ensnared by his fear. But seeing this girl who was even more afraid than himself made Gene feel something he couldn't explain. He wished he could do something to help her.

"Where's your family?" he said.

When she offered only tears, Gene began his own story, focusing mostly on the man. But the way Gene described him gave the impression that he'd mistaken a nightmare for reality. The girl didn't ask questions, Gene desperately hoping she would believe him. He wanted all of these kids to believe him. They were in danger, even with the door locked, Rock having told them they were safe as long as they stayed put.

But they weren't safe anywhere. The man would come – Gene knew it absolutely. As long as Gene was in this classroom, the bloody X stinging beneath the bandage, the man would come for him.

"Where do you–?" Gene began, but a long round of pops echoed from somewhere below, vibrations tremoring lightly up the walls.

Gene had only heard gunfire in movies, sneaking downstairs sometimes after his parents put him to bed, but he was confident that these sounds came from guns. Big guns.

Listening closely, Gene could hear screaming interspersed among the shots. The screams sounded hollow and distorted, as if projected from a distant loudspeaker, but soon the chaos ceased altogether.

There was an apprehensive silence, most of the kids shrinking back from the door. One boy remained, his breath fogging up the glass.

Gene and the little girl matched each other's fearful stares. Still no adults returned, and Gene's terror grew like a midday desert sun, inescapable, his heart crashing against his chest, his hands slick with sweat. He just knew he'd see that awful hooded face again – any second it would be at the window, recessed eyes tracing the little faces in search of one boy, the one with the X upon his forehead.

He's coming! He's coming soon!

No one would understand because they hadn't seen him, but the man was coming. He was approaching fast, and Gene was scared, too scared, starting to shake now, his thoughts shifting to where the man might take him and what he planned to do to him. There would be a cave somewhere, dark and drippy, or a vulture's nest and a dozen beaks ready to pick him apart, or a pit with snakes like the one in the last movie Mom and Dad had watched.

Yes, the man would take Gene to a place like that – a place where the sun never shined – and then, only then, would he carve Gene up into little pieces and squirt some ketchup onto them and gobble them up with yellow-black teeth.

Gene could hear the man's words, over and over and over. As if spoken just a moment ago, they skittered coldly around Gene's head and made him repeatedly glance at the door.

Eventually, inevitably, as though Gene's obsessive fears had produced it, the terrible face appeared at the window, peeking in – except it wasn't the man's face but a mask.

The door handle jiggled insistently. "Let me in, kids," came a man's voice from behind what appeared to be a tiger mask.

BLAZE THE GRID

The red-haired boy who'd been glued to the glass was now staggering backward, tripping over a cot. The girl seated beside Gene mumbled senseless words of fear, her complexion snowing over.

"Let me in, little ones," the man called, his striped mask tilted slightly, Gene positive that the guy beneath it was staring directly at him. Was it *him*?

When no one moved, the man slammed against the door. "Let me in, you little bastards, or I'll rip your heads off when I get in there! Every last one of you!"

Chaos ensued, kids crying and stumbling and hiding, but quickly the assaults of the door yielded to silence. The hallway was empty again.

This time it was Gene who approached the door, his steps impossibly small, his body weighed down by the fear of what he knew he'd see out there in the hallway.

But he needed to do this. He needed to check.

Chapter 2

"Come with us," the leader of the camouflaged snipers urged. "We can't waste time talking."

A small, boxy man with a thin mustache, the leader looked like someone you might encounter at an art museum or a poetry reading at a coffee house. He reminded Tommy Sims of an English teacher who'd been a colleague back on the other side of the bridge, when people had still driven vehicles. This English teacher, known even to other faculty members as Mr. Keating, had dyed his mustache and hair uncompromisingly black, not intending to resemble a vampire, but the combination of that relentless dye job and his pale complexion had made it unavoidable.

"He looks like Mr. Keating," Tommy said, speaking to no one. It was all he could do to keep from looking at the dead men pooled in blood.

"How do we know we can trust you people?" Dominick Sims said, shocked by how rapidly life had crumbled. Just a few hours ago they'd been on their way to Lake Lashaway to set up a bonfire and look out at the water and remember how things once were. Then Dom's car had shut down on Route 49, dump trucks arriving minutes later to clear away every stalled vehicle. Later, Dom and Tommy had been imprisoned by a Bible-thumping, bunker-building lunatic who'd subsequently been massacred along with his supporters – massacred by these men now standing before them.

"You guys killed a cop," Beatrice said, her eyes glazed with shock. "Or at least he's dressed like a cop."

"It's every man for himself now," Bea's father said, pushing his wheelchair up beside her. "Those men were corrupt, evil – can't believe Tim got caught up with them."

The little mustached man, scarcely 5'5'', consulted a GIS accureader and then spoke calmly into his radio, providing their coordinates and asking how far out the bus was. These men were so well concealed by their camouflage fatigues that, when they'd first emerged after shooting Pastor Tim Thorne and the others, it had seemed as though the trees were approaching.

Tommy, powerless to control his wandering eyes, was overwhelmed by the mass grave before him. Another group of fighter jets roared overhead, as if to remind Tommy that the world wasn't what it had been a few hours ago. Mr. Keating might well be dead, the shine finally to fade from his hair and mustache, and what about Tommy's parents? What about family and friends? There was no way to reach anyone, no way to find out if they were okay.

"You didn't have to kill them!" Tommy shouted, not realizing how close he'd gotten to the men until he felt Dom and Bea holding him back.

"Believe me, mister, we had to put 'em down," the mustached man said, his tone strangely flat.

"Tommy, please don't do this," Bea said. "Let's just get out of here. We're all in danger."

***

"Thanks again for finishing those bastards," Sherman "Steel" Sparks said, shaking the men's hands again. "Saved our asses."

Virgil offered a quick nod. "Sure thing. You boys were like squirrels on a low branch, just fixing to get yourselves hunted down. Figured we best get in there before bad became worse."

Having walked a short distance east to check the enemy's vehicles for weapons, they now stood between two black vans. Parked at the periphery of the chaos, well beyond the other vans and the overturned trailer, these vehicles hadn't sustained any damage from the shootout.

As shaky as a man in withdrawal, flinching at every sound – especially the frequent air traffic – Paul Shannon couldn't believe the amount of weaponry the men discovered in the vans. They were loaded with machine guns and semiautomatic weapons, even a pair of rocket launchers. Along the walls of each modified utility van, stored in cabinets, was enough ammunition to supply an army.

"We need to get back to base before more of them come," Virgil said, even though his men wanted to search the other vans.

Steel armed himself with fresh confidence in the form of a machine gun, the ammo belt coiled around him like a massive snake. Paul lowered his head and prayed for his family back home in Chicago.

Virgil pointed to the vans. "You guys drive these and follow us," he told Paul and Steel. "I'll have some people trail you. I'll feel a lot better once we get back to 148. We've got guys securing that road."

As if someone had pressed fast-forward and sped Paul along through the minutes, he was suddenly alone behind the wheel of one of the vans, driving for the first time since he was a teenager, determined to keep up with the rest of the group. Steel's van was immediately in front of him on Route 9, six motorcycles spaced out behind him.

The lane seemed strangely thin, as though Paul were trying to navigate a curving bowling lane. He kept both hands on the wheel, eyes locked straight ahead, though they occasionally darted in the direction of a fire or a smash-up.

A few enemy vans and trucks passed in the other direction, Paul fearing another battle, but apparently a brief stalemate had been earned. Perhaps enemy scouts had already reported the defeat that had just been dealt by the Freedom Riders. Or maybe these were simply transport minions tasked with assisting the destruction teams.

Around the next curve, the motorcycles in front of Paul slowed and banked left onto Route 148. Fortifications had been arranged on the Brookfield Town Common out of wrecked vehicles and a few school buses; gunners were likely shielded behind them, their motorcycles parked around the gazebo.

Paul, spotting two snipers walking along the roof of the library beyond the southeastern edge of the Common, pictured Steel's map in his head and tried to figure out how long it would take them to reach the school. If you were to draw a square in south central Massachusetts, Route 9 would be your ceiling, Route 20 your floor, Route 49 forming the right wall, and Route 148 on the left.

And how many were dead within that blasted square? How many were suffering, separated from their families, unable to find help?

Their unlikely convoy was headed south now on Route 148, climbing a short hill and crossing a railroad overpass, heavy train traffic below. Paul hadn't gotten a great look, but he thought he'd glimpsed trains moving in both directions.

Have they taken over the railroads, too? How have they managed all of this so quickly?

Him! It must be him. He's assembled the demons and the damned.

The houses and businesses on Route 148 were untouched. Nothing burned. Nothing had been destroyed. Vehicles remained where they'd been when the grid stopped: a pickup truck that had been pulling out of a driveway was frozen mid-turn in the northbound lane; farther south, a little hydrocar sat with all four doors open. Having abandoned hope of the grid powering up again, stranded travelers had departed on foot hours earlier.

With only himself to rely on for conversation, Paul let prayer guide him through the southbound minutes, the houses on either side of the road soon giving way to woods, the obstacle course of vehicles thinning. At first Paul's prayers brought him comfort and relative calm, but after a while he began to feel empty and alone, reminded of another time when his desperate prayers had gone unanswered.

Chicago. He'd been seventeen years and four months old. It had been April in the Windy City, time for basketball on the outdoor courts with his friends again, though you had to layer up at night and the shovels were sometimes needed. Graduation had been a wink away, Paul's letter of intent to the University of Kentucky having been signed back in February, a high school sectional championship celebrated in March. Everything was fresh and hopeful that spring, until one night driving home Paul's vision went a little gleamy, headlights and streetlights a touch too twinkly. Later, toward the end of the trip, some of the oncoming headlights banded together in coronas, others strangely bright and misshapen.

Paul thought little of the oddness at first – just tired, that's all. But his vision faltered again the next night, and that's when he started to get scared, remembering his late grandfather's curse. Almost two weeks later he woke from a nightmare to a bedroom that was tomb black, even with moonlight spilling in. Outside, the neighborhood seemed to have experienced a power outage, except a few windows in the nearest house shined in odd, spectral whitish light, pale and shallow, like a faint glow beneath the surface of a lake.

Paul knew right then, choking on realization, that it had come for him, the curse climbing down from the torchlit stagecoach of nightmares and coming to claim him in the waking world, just as it had come for his grandfather.

Searching through his bedroom window, Paul thought for just a moment he saw a silhouette shifting in the wicked darkness. The curse was waiting out there in the infinite ocean that should have been a moonlit, streetlit driveway, only a few lights bobbing on that too-black sea.

Panicking, Paul stared down at his blackened blankets, clasped his hands together, and prayed aloud. He didn't want to close his eyes for even a second; if he closed his eyes, it would get him, he feared, that faceless phantom he'd seen in nightmares. It had been creeping up on him for years – closer, closer, closest when he slept – and now the menace was just outside, waiting. Paul feared he'd be blind by morning if he slept, and not only would his vision depart but so, too, would his aspirations. His future. His life.

Breaking out in sweat, rubbing his eyes fiercely, Paul began to pace the room with building nausea. He prayed for it to not be happening as it had happened to his grandfather – *Please, God, don't make me live in the dark. Don't take my eyes.*

BLAZE THE GRID

Paul's prayers seemed to find an answer, the neighborhood gradually coming back into partial clarity as the first lights of sunrise slipped in from the east. It was enough for Paul to understand that the swaying silhouette from the previous night had not belonged to a specter but instead one of the trash cans stacked along his neighbor's fence. Yes, of course, that was where the trash cans were always kept, but nothing had been the same when Paul's world went dark, only a few lights of hope left on as the curse drew far too close.

Paul was free of The Curse for a few nights – he kept trying to push his symptoms aside as overtiredness – but by the weekend T.C. was rolling back into town again on its stagecoach, clattering along the cobblestones of Paul's dread-razed mind, threatening him once more with the image of a coal-dark neighborhood.

This time Paul staggered down the black hole of his second-floor hallway, tears in his eyes, hands groping for the banister, crying out, feeling like a child. His parents took him to the hospital, Paul keeping his eyes shut on the way, hoping to blot out the truth.

I'll see again when we get there. It will all be normal again.

And it was normal again. In the brightly lit hospital, The Curse was chased back to its shadow stallions, which chuffed and clopped somewhere out there in the infinite distance, grinning, knowing. Their driver was not yet strong enough to fully penetrate the light, though Paul's specialists later warned that the disease would worsen…and that nothing could be done about it.

T.C. would come again one night, but it wouldn't linger outside this time. It would break in. It would loom at the foot of the bed, and then, maybe the next night, it would take everything.

Paul's hopelessness had been the worst part, like being tied to the train tracks and waiting for a headlight to appear on the horizon.

Paul began to miss school. His grades declined. Eventually forced to inform his college of what was happening, it seemed a letter would arrive any day announcing that his scholarship had been rescinded. He feared that every pushup and sprint had been for nothing, that every extra shot after practice had been a waste. His parents were constantly at his side as spring wore on, especially at night, setting up sleeping bags and hugging him through it when he awoke afraid to open his eyes and enter the world lorded by The Curse between suns. It was always worse at night, much worse. There were flashlights and prayers. They kept the lights on. And The Curse got a little closer every night – and a little bolder.

Paul prayed often with his family. Their pastor gave him a special prayer one rainy Sunday morning at church, only a few hours after The Curse rode off into the dying darkness, Paul's vision coming limply back around…but one day soon it would be gone for good, stolen and stashed aboard the shadowy stagecoach. Meantime, the parishioners sang uplifting songs and praised the Lord and His light, their prayers useless against the darkness.

BLAZE THE GRID

It happened like that for roughly two months, an agonizing pattern, every day seeming to lose a minute or two to the bad side, darkness coming a little earlier and departing a little later. The photoreceptor cells in Paul's retinas were under constant attack, reducing his vision to a steadily narrowing tunnel, The Curse always waiting at its end. He was allowed to finish school online. His girlfriend dumped him, said she had to focus on her future. He struggled at basketball, kept missing easy shots, the hoop a blurry moving target; sometimes he just stood in the middle of the court and dribbled with his eyes closed, remembering. His parents tried to offer inspiration, but what could they do when even the doctors couldn't stop those dreaded wagon wheels from clattering in?

Paul started off light with alcohol, then got a little heavier. Weeks passed. He snuck out of his house one evening, his peripheral vision destroyed by then, confining him to the narrow tunnel even by day. And the nights were black, unendurable terrors unless he had a little help to get him through.

That particular evening in July, impaled by the fork of despair – a fork twirled gleefully by T.C. – Paul took a half-drunken walk to the bus stop, a bottle of whiskey in his shorts pocket. The bus brought him across town, where he found himself walking alongside the windy canal, Chicago alive with sound and burnt, strange light that coruscated off buildings. Monolithic shadows flared up all around, the skyscrapers like clouds of whirling smoke.

It was quickly getting darker. Too quickly.

Disoriented and scared when his vision accelerated its customary nightly fade to watercolor blurs, Paul contemplated returning home around eight. Glancing frequently behind him, he kept thinking he heard wagon wheels in the distance, clattering above the traffic.

It's coming again. It'll be real bad tonight.

Oblivious to Paul's distress, the city bustled around him. A hotel domineered to his left, its sign too blurry to read, its guests faceless. The canal should have been a postcard for him to enjoy at this hour, the water resplendent in its ever-changing shades of blue, the skyscrapers gilded at sunset like pyramids – yet Paul had to rely on his imagination to see past the muddled ruin the world had become.

Walking defiantly on, taking a few swigs of whiskey, losing himself to the sounds of the city, Paul remembered countless Bulls games with his father, remembered thinking that maybe he'd be there one day, putting up numbers like Jordan, or at least wowing some kid watching March Madness. He would be on ESPN one day – that's what he'd told his father. One day they would all know Paul Shannon's name.

A mile farther, the basketball courts were full of distorted shadows backlit by skeins of twilight. Paul knew somebody had made a shot from the sound, not the sight, and the roads were like images of time-lapse traffic, streaks of dull red and white stretching into the distance. He had to be especially careful at the crosswalks, straining what was left of his vision but mostly relying on his hearing.

And yet again Paul thought he heard it over the hum of traffic – a baleful sound amidst the city's cacophony. Wagon wheels behind him, a little closer than they'd been before.

Paul stopped, listened. Shadows and shapes slipped past. An invisible subway rattled overhead, drowning the wagon wheels, but when Paul resumed walking the sounds continued their pursuit.

It's nothing, just the whiskey. Keep moving.

On he walked, venturing through one intersection after another, all the way to the Navy Pier, tired of being afraid – and fuck it, he could walk these streets in his sleep. He wouldn't be chased home. Another swig. This was his town! But…

They were dim and scattered like sparks, those Navy Pier Ferris wheel lights, and Paul's eyes were fresh with tears as he stepped closer and gazed up at the big wheel, letting it gleam brightly in his memory. There were people all around him, families and couples and friends, everyone having fun, laughing, talking excitedly about the imminent fireworks, oblivious to the young man in their midst whose life was crumbling.

Why me? Of all these people, why does it have to be me, God?

Paul remembered the joy he'd felt on signing the commitment letter to Kentucky. His father had said he would make it big. His mother had never looked prouder. He'd thought he was on his way.

"It's not supposed to be like this."

Paul was squeezing the steering wheel, so lost in memory that he nearly rammed into Steel's van when it slowed around a bend. The clouds were reconvening, a heavy wall of late November gray spreading across the afternoon sky, leaving the road dark enough for headlights.

The rest of the trip Paul spent wondering about his purpose. That his vision had been restored now of all times was well beyond coincidence, but what was he to do? Seeing the suffering did not empower him to stop it. He was just another witness, just another survivor trying to avoid becoming a victim.

Paul was deep in prayer by the time they made a right into Tantasqua High School, a sprawling building set well back from the road, a little pond and a football field up front, the baseball diamond settled at the finish of a sharp slope that tumbled down from the entry road.

The parking lots were overflowing with hundreds of motorcycles, some left on the grassy medians between lots and the walkway off the bus disembarkment circle. Men and women with guns let them through a series of gates, until finally they were entering the school.

"What shape's Route 9 in?" a man asked Virgil in the crowded atrium.

Virgil shook his head. "They've got heavy traffic out there. We took a few out, recovered an impressive weapons cache. We'll be in good shape to defend this place tonight, but let's hope those reinforcements from Westover get here by morning."

Tonight???

Steel's eyes tracked to the front doors and beyond, where it was dark outside, but surely even the fiercest clouds couldn't bring such an eclipse.

"Paul!" Steel began, but a rage of gunfire derailed the words ready to follow.

Chapter 3

By the time Harry Freed boarded the van, he was exhausted from the walk through the woods and his sickness.

Through the window of the van, Harry watched helplessly as the Perron and DiMarteer houses burned, the flames having ridden the wind across the street and set two more houses ablaze, as well as the adjacent woods. Soon the whole neighborhood would be consumed in a wildfire to rival those out west, and no one was coming to extinguish it.

Harry couldn't believe how lucky he'd been to find the van. After realizing the futility in attempting to rescue residents who might have been trapped in the engulfed houses, Harry had stumbled down the street to Brookfield Road. The van, a rusted senior center shuttle bus, had come not a minute later.

Now Harry was sitting beside a stranger named Dominick Sims; his brother Tommy Sims and several others were on board as well. Their stories ranged from shocking to maddening, each one adding another lurid hue to a portrait of chaos. The idea that it had all been carefully orchestrated got Harry feeling even more lightheaded, about ready to bloody faint.

"My sons are in New York and Philly. Do you think it's spread that far?" Harry said.

"It's happening across the country," a man in the opposite aisle said, his wife seated beside him. "I've been in radio contact all night with people nationwide. They're building a wall down south, God knows why."

Harry nodded thinly, sickened by his inability to contact his sons. "That Freedom Riders guy" – he pointed to the front of the vehicle at a man wearing a bandana who'd first invited him aboard – "he said the attack might be a collaboration between several countries."

"Whoever's doing this, we'll lay them out by morning," Dominick said. "Once they get the armies mobilized, these bastards are dead."

Harry wished Dominick's optimism were contagious. He'd just dreamt of dystopia – a totalitarian adolescent regime – and now, impossibly, society had degraded overnight into something far worse. None of the passengers' faces were aglow with electronic devices. No one spoke on their phones, instead staring out the windows with fear-washed expressions.

Harry closed his eyes, fearing for his sons and their families. He'd read enough novels and seen enough movies to know that cities were the worst places to be in times of catastrophe. Too many people, too few exits. The tunnels and bridges that fed life into New York would be snarled and strangled, utterly gridlocked now that Devlin's dream had failed. A little south, Philly would be only slightly less difficult to escape.

"Almost there, folks," announced the man with the bandana up front.

The other Freedom Riders who'd rescued them occupied the first rows of seats. There were apparently dozens of rescue vans like this one fanned out across the region, some accompanied by the National Guard. Most of the vans were headed for Tantasqua High School.

Harry prayed for those who hadn't been rescued yet. Whoever was left out there tonight, where flames lorded with impunity and smoke skated along the wind – whoever was still out there was as good as dead.

***

Even the choking grip of fear couldn't prevent Tommy's sleep.

Bea's head propped lightly against his shoulder, the van humming along Brookfield Road, Tommy slipped away for a time. And when he reached that place where visions awaited, a lion mask came to him in vivid detail – but also the boy behind that mask. He was maybe nine or ten years old, a boy with tears and fear and hatred in his eyes, blood on his fattened lip. He was curled up on a bed, knees to chin, covering his ears with clenched fists, and Tommy could feel the rage that diseased him.

Quickly the vision alternated between images of the boy with and without his mask on, in one moment carrying a pistol and the next cowering on his bed. There was a name edging in from the periphery, but it wouldn't introduce itself, not yet, Tommy aching with pity for this boy he did not know, wishing to quell his pain.

Suddenly the kid was gone altogether, a new vision taking Tommy back to Route 49, where a stagecoach was on fire, its driver repeatedly cracking a whip across the backs of massive black horses. They were going far too fast around a curve, the coach overturning, Tommy tumbling out of the vision as if he'd been a passenger inside the coach.

Tommy jolted free of sleep, waking Bea in the process.

"Sorry," he murmured, settling a hand on her arm. "Bad dream."

She looked over at him, eyes wide in the mostly dark van; dim aisle lights sprinkled a ghostly glow over the other weary faces.

"Another vision?" Bea said, leaning in.

"Yeah, but I don't know if I can figure this one out."

He told her about it, half-expecting Bea to solve it for him. Perhaps it had simply been a senseless nightmare and not a vision, except the haunted look in that boy's eyes had reached deep within Tommy and wouldn't let go. The boy was out there somewhere, Tommy sensed, probably wearing his mask at that very moment – but what was the significance? And how did it connect to a flaming stagecoach rattling down Route 49?

"It's amazing," Bea said after Tommy finished describing what he'd seen. She took his hand and rested against him once more, Tommy startled by an urge to kiss her. "All of these things happening tonight, first your ability to walk again and now the visions. What if you were, I don't know…chosen or something?"

Tommy chuckled. "Then I'd say God picked the wrong guy. He should have chosen someone a lot braver than me."

"But God doesn't make mistakes." She squeezed his hand. "This is a gift, Tommy – a miracle. You could save us."

He nodded to the front of the van. "Those guys save people, not me. My visions will probably end up getting us all killed."

"Have a little faith." She spoke very softly now, and with greater urgency. "It might not seem like there's a plan, but there is a plan for you, Tommy, a plan for all of us."

"That's what your pastor thought, too. He had a perfectly good plan…and he wound up dead."

Tommy was still reliving the final moments for Timothy Thorne and his son and his men. It was surprising that their lifeless faces hadn't stared emptily in Tommy's nightmare; instead, a masked boy and a fiery stagecoach had inhabited his latest visions.

"Pastor Tim lost it," Bea whispered. "He let himself be ruled by fear. He tried to control everyone instead of working as a team." She sighed at length.

"It's gonna get worse before it gets better – a lot worse. We all have to stay together."

Tommy was shocked to discover his lips briefly upon hers. Bea was momentarily frozen, unblinking, speechless, her lips slightly parted. Tommy grew convinced that she would recede, but instead she closed the space between them this time.

The other hushed conversations fell rapidly away, and now it was just him and Beatrice, the woman he'd met as the houses burned.

***

Even though Tantasqua High School was lit up in the distance like an airport, Harry didn't notice the building as they pulled into the entry road.

His mind was far away, lost again in a moment that had left him broken. He couldn't quite remember what the doctor had looked like, only what he'd said, that his wife was responding well to a new cancer treatment after years of battling. Harry had felt an immense weight fly off, but just a few days later poor Janey's decline had been incomprehensibly quick. A severe infection, the doctors said, and a week later she was gone.

Harry spent months in a disbelieving haze, waking every morning with the expectation of seeing Janey beside him, unable to accept that he was all alone. Wanting to keep Janey close and remember some of the best times, Harry bought himself a ticket to a Red Sox game that summer, but the stranger's face in the next seat caused Harry to be chased from the game faster than the visiting pitcher…and the bloke's ERA was real lousy, somewhere north of 6.00.

Even the ballgames on TV were spurious and empty without Janey, no one there to share stories with and laugh with and eat popcorn with. And why hadn't those bloody doctors been able to do a thing to help her? They'd built Harry up with hope and then let him crash – a bunch of plungelickers, as Harry's students would say – and he hadn't known what to do with himself after his sweet Janey was gone. Maybe he would take out election papers and vie for a seat on the Board of This-or-That. Maybe he'd join an astronomy club and look at the stars, see if he could glimpse Janey twinkling up there. Maybe he'd do a little golfing during the next thunderstorm and hopefully reserve a place of his own in the lovely firmament.

Those doctors really had been bloody useless bastards.

The van came to a stop, Harry jarred free of his memories. The school was to his right, a mammoth of a building he'd visited half a dozen times to cast his vote at town elections. The regional school served students from five towns, and if you walked to the end of every hall you just might cross the border into each town.

The van's doors cranked open, the Riders hopping down with their guns, the driver reminding passengers that they would all be assigned a job once inside. The Riders' calmness amid chaos wasn't a surprise, most of them having fought in wars no one had cared much about. To serve in an unpopular war was bad enough, but to have hardly anyone even remember your war, to face death every day in service to your country and have kids twenty years later wonder how exactly wounded warriors had been wounded – *that*, Harry felt, was the ultimate insult.

And how could the kids be faulted? When you're breastfed by technology, how can you be expected to notice anything beyond the screen? And when adults forfeit driving due to the lure of increased safety/productivity/efficiency/fun, what will they do when the system fails?

"Who drives us now that the grid is gone?" Harry muttered as he passed through the front doors of TRHS, home of the Warriors, where a school play had been set for the weekend, student performers ready to present Virgil and Beatrice and the countless hellish creatures of *Dante's Inferno*.

Chapter 4

Amie Valenzuela, who'd been sitting toward the back of the pre-grid shuttle van with Jazzi, limped into the high school with her family. Her injuries from earlier – *Stop resisting!* – were collecting an even steeper toll now that she'd followed her parents for two miles through the woods before coming to a road, terror shadowing every step.

Amie's parents and grandparents, along with several other passengers fresh off the van, were forced to relinquish their weapons after passing beneath SchoolSafe scanners. The outer perimeter weapons detectors had been deactivated to prevent the SchoolSafe shields from automatically sealing off the building, but the interior scanners chimed at almost every entrant.

Beyond the initial security stations, newcomers darted about the atrium in panicked search of loved ones. The military had teamed up with the Freedom Riders to bring the school into relative order, and they patiently provided directions to crying parents and lost children and injured seniors.

Amie stayed behind her parents with Jazzi, holding hands, trying to breathe deeply against the claustrophobia. She searched the frantic crowd for Xeke, thinking a few times that she'd picked his face out from hundreds. She was wrong on each occasion.

"I don't like this, Amie." Jazzi looked worriedly up at her. "Too many people."

Amie kneeled. "I don't like it either, but this is just the entrance. It'll be better soon, I promise."

Jazzi began searching as well, her eyes scampering about, but she had no greater luck in finding Sena than Amie had in locating Xeke.

At last they were herded along, Grandpa having argued about being forced to give up his gun, Mom and Dad urging him to comply.

"This is a horrible idea – now we're defenseless!" Grandpa shouted.

"You'll be safe here, sir," a woman responded from the ruck behind them.

"Safe, my ass!" Grandpa wheeled around in search of the woman, a vein throbbing in his forehead. "This is a goddamn war! Every single one of us is a soldier!"

Chapter 5

Dalton Rose was brought to a new room on the second floor. Dusty, with his puffball white hair and trenchant eyes, reminded Dalton often of what would be done to him if he didn't comply.

"You must give yourself to us, Rosey, and in return we will give you the world," Dusty said, standing at the head of the classroom and looking down at Dalton in a front row desk. Somehow he knew Dalton's nickname, which was frenny but also reassuring. Things had changed. Impossibilities had become very possible. And now it was finally time for others to know the pain.

Dalton's mouth throbbed, his teeth sensitive to every breath. Dusty had stabbed him in the shoulder with a syringe and injected him with something frennylicious, Dalton doubting his promises of relief. But the pain really had lessened, to the point that Dalton could move his mouth a little, his jaw loose and saggy, unhinged like a broken door…and the blood kept leaking down his chin and draining back into his throat, over and over and over, every swallow a burning tempest. His whole face felt puffy, but at least the agony had come down from its summit.

"Soon you won't need that thing at all," Dusty said, eyeing the device Dalton had been given to communicate. "Of course, assuming you perform."

The creeper was gone a moment later, not walking off but vanishing, silence sliding in, Dalton cobwebbed with surreal consternation. He focused on his breathing, slow and slower. He cursed his uncle.

He got me into this. He knew this would happen. I shouldn't have listened.

Uncle Ed had been acting spurdog all week, beginning late Monday night when Dalton, on his way downstairs from his room, had stopped at the railing, watching as his uncle paced the foyer below and whispered to himself, at times mumbling, at times grunting and growling.

Shrinking back from the railing, listening as the strangeness continued, Dalton wondered if Uncle Ed had started drinking again. He could sometimes go dry for a few months, never without self-praise, but he always ended up in the drink again. Depression was usually his excuse, his life scrambled ever since Aunt Jo left. Their three kids were in college or the workforce, Dalton the only kid left at home, not that this was his home or he was Uncle Ed's kid – it was just a place he'd gone after Dad killed Mom.

Uncle Ed. He wasn't the worst guy, striving constantly to compensate for his busted interior with a glowing exterior. Dalton could strongly relate; sometimes there was no fixing what lurked inside. You just had to throw something over it, cover it up, pretend it wasn't there, and never listen to that fucking song again, Volbeat's "Heaven nor Hell", once a favorite and now the plague – the song that had drowned his ears when Mom needed him most.

Uncle Ed kept the poodyloose going for the rest of the week. Tuesday night he was bombed and carefree, asking Dalton to join him for shots at the basement bar. Wednesday he was manic, taking a two-hour bike ride and then stuffing himself with microwavable pies.

On Thursday, Uncle Ed ordered Dalton to skip school the next day and pack for an extended trip. Dalton's questions were carefully dodged, Uncle Ed repeatedly urging him to pack anything of significance. Dalton knew better than to continue pressing; it was obvious that his uncle had gotten hooked up in something septic at work. Maybe he'd rebelled against his employer, the Department of Compliance and Exemptions, but why didn't COMPLEX just give him the axe? Why was he running?

Had Dalton known then where his uncle's plans would lead, he would have been out of the state by now.

Instead he sat at a desk on the second floor of Tantasqua HS, holding his jaw steady. After a while Dusty returned with a middle-aged guy in handcuffs. He was bald, sweating profusely, his face bloody, but at least he had his teeth.

"Please don't do this," the man panted. "I'm begging you – I have a family."

Dusty shoved a pistol into the man's side. Someone snapped the door shut behind them, and now it was just the three of them.

The handcuffed man's gaze flashed to Dalton, whereupon a broader horror barreled into his eyes, as though he were a little boy who'd glimpsed a grinning clown beneath his bed. "Please don't hurt me, kid. Whatever they told you – it's a lie! It's all a lie!"

"Down," Dusty calmly ordered. "To your knees."

The man's eyes shifted to Dusty, then angled imploringly back to Dalton. The sight of him battered and broken made Dalton queasy.

"Down," Dusty said again, sounding bored. With cracking knees and a wince the man kneeled. "Good. Very good." Dusty came up the aisle beside Dalton and opened his trench coat. "Here you are, Rosey." He presented an assault rifle and a lion mask, leaving the latter on the desk.

What do you want? Dalton said by typing into the device.

"What do you think?" Dusty nodded at the rifle Dalton refused to take. "You're going to shoot that man dead, Rosey."

Dalton recoiled, the device tumbling with a clatter onto the desk. For a moment he felt unreal, as if he were comprised entirely of vapor. Forgetting the device, he began to speak, but he could only manage a single word before the pain halted him, lashing out from his jaw and ricocheting around his mouth.

He grabbed up the device. *I won't*. When Dusty said nothing: *You're not serious.*

Dusty took a tour of the room, glancing casually at posters, touching a few of them, all while a sickening dread pressurized Dalton's chest. He kept locking stares with the man in handcuffs, the blazing desperation in his eyes making Dalton feel even more septic.

Eventually Dusty settled into the teacher's chair, behind a desk cluttered with books and folders and other school shit. He swung his leather boots up onto the desk, a few books crashing to the floor. "You're going to shoot that man dead, Rosey." He pointed at Dalton. "Don't you want to hurt Xeke Hamilton? Don't you want to make them all pay for what they did to you? This is the first step – you must prove yourself."

Dalton blinked at him. His rage had come down from the boil, but even at its worst he knew he couldn't have shot a defenseless man. There was vengeance, and then there was insanity, Dalton starting to sweat because he feared he wouldn't be given a choice between the two.

"Please!" the man begged, shaking his handcuffs out in front of him. "Please, kid, I have a family! Don't do this!"

"Relax," Dalton managed, and this time there was far less pain than before. "I. Won't. Hurt. You." He spoke thinly, expecting with each word a renewed agony, his lips weirdly flappy now that most of his front teeth were gone. That moment when the gun had shattered his teeth – it kept replaying in Dalton's head, making him cringe.

Anger flickered into Dusty's eyes. Back on his feet, he crossed the room to Dalton and offered the rifle once more. "Put the mask on and take this gun! Take it!" Spit flew from his mouth. "Do it now, or I'll let them have you. There will be no hope for you, boy. None!"

Dalton scooped up the lion mask from the desk. He was about to toss it at Dusty and leave the room, but the lights failed, dipping them in darkness that wasn't quite absolute. Tiny lights came from above, glimmering like stars, but they weren't stars – they were snowflakes, glowing softly as they drifted down.

"What the fuck?" the man in handcuffs said.

The snowflakes melted on contact, Dalton leaping up in atavistic response, suddenly knowing what was happening, even before the lights returned to reveal a new setting.

Dalton collapsed to his knees, tears in his eyes. The classroom had become an emergency room – *the* emergency room. Dusty and his prisoner were gone, replaced by a pair of nurses whose eyes glossed over Dalton as they passed him.

The gun was gone. The mask was gone. The pain was completely gone.

"Please, God, no." Dalton could feel his teeth clicking together as he ran – teeth that hadn't been there a few seconds ago.

He launched around a corner, staggered right, and arrived outside the curtained cubicle where he'd been taken that Christmas Eve. He rushed through a series of doors, but they all led back to the same ER cubicle.

The lights fell away, only the curtains aglow.

"Kill him," came a distant whisper. "Kill him and rise. End your suffering. Make them pay. Take your army. It is time, Dalton Rose."

Dalton wobbled incredulously, wondering if it was all a hallucination. Yes, it had to be. The syringe. Dusty had injected him with something frennylicious, maybe one of those new Leapland drugs they'd come out with, the shit those kids from Springfield took last year down in the MSR, made them eat their friends' faces off.

Dalton stilled himself, ignoring the rising, ghoulish moans beyond the curtain to his right. They emanated from the woman who'd gone forever faceless, the one Dalton had thought was Mom. He still dreamed of that woman suffering in obscurity on Christmas Eve. He was much braver in his dreams, sometimes reaching steadily for the curtain, intent on pulling it aside, yet he always lurched awake before he saw her face.

"Help me," the woman called from within the chalky glow of the curtain, and this time it wasn't a dream.

"Please help me."

Every cell, every platelet, every molecule froze, paralyzing Dalton. All he could do was stare at the softly fluttering luminescent curtain and listen to the pleading voice behind it. For a moment he thought he could make out a silhouette – someone sitting on the bed, arms extended.

"Help me, Dalton. Help me." The voice was louder now, Dalton clenching his fists. His head began to pulse, and he felt like he was very slowly melting down, hot-cold and septic, fucking harrowed, scrambled, blasted.

His teeth chattered. He felt even colder, creaky and sick and frigid. He bent over, clutched his stomach, wondering if he might puke. Still the woman was calling to him, but then Mom's voice rang out, frail and choked.

"Help me, baby! Please, just turn your music off!"

Dalton covered his eyes, thinking he'd seen someone just behind the curtain, a shadow hand pushing it outward.

It's just the drugs! It's not real!

"Turn your music off! I'll die if you don't help me!" and she said his name, his real name.

Dalton could hear the music now, at first light like elevator music but quickly crisp and resonant. It was "Heaven nor Hell", of course it was, the harmonica notes like shrapnel exploding through him, dropping him flat, louder and louder and louder, crushing him and forcing him to remember…

…Their shouting voices had always rattled through the walls and Dalton's bones, leaving him shuddery and fearful, but his music had gotten him through it, heavy metal until the fighting stopped, until there was quiet, Dad down to the basement, Mom left broken somewhere, usually hurrying to her bedroom so Dalton wouldn't find her like that. Eventually she came to his room and hugged him, read to him, watched movies with him.

But not that night. Not that Christmas Eve…"Heaven nor Hell" had ended – *I saw an angel become the Devil* – and Dalton had stared at the locked door with an almost preternatural dread after his father had stopped shouting for him to open it. Only the soughing wind had broken a baleful winter silence, the Christmas tree glowing downstairs for the final time.

Dalton had waited as he always did, waited and waited for his mother to come get him, then waited some more. Surely the weak knocks upon his door would come any second, but they never did. Instead there were men's voices and thudding footsteps downstairs a while later that metalized Dalton's marrow, forcing him to hide in his closet.

BLAZE THE GRID

A neighbor had called 911 and reported a commotion. Dalton's mother had been found dead, his father arrested, and his bedroom door had come crashing in that Christmas Eve. He remembered nothing of the subsequent trip to the hospital, only what they told him once he was there, in the cubicle.

Dalton pushed himself up against the weight of the music, the decibels like bricks. Blue and violet strobe lights spiraled through the derangement, making him dizzy, funneling his vision to the floor, where the assault rifle and the mask waited.

"Blaze him, Dalton!" Dusty shouted. "Make him pay! He should be dead, not in jail!"

Straight ahead, the strobes were whittled down to blue shafts converging into a single spotlight, Dalton's father blinking out into the surrounding darkness like a blind man. He wore a DOC jumpsuit, the spotlight following him as he shuffled lightly in clinking leg restraints.

Dalton lifted the gun, unable to steady it with trembling hands. Something beyond hatred, burning and infinite, took him then, helped him level the gun.

"I love you, Mom," he rasped.

Dalton fired until his father's orange jumpsuit was mostly red. Staring at the mutilated corpse, he grinned with the realization that he would make this aspect of the hallucination real.

Soon he would be free.

Soon there would be pain.

Until then, he put on the mask, sat against the wall, and invited the darkness. He didn't have to wait long before the curtain slid gently back.

BLAZE THE GRID

Chapter 6

Death takes a final inventory of his arrangements.

The window is closing, but the preparations have been made. Soon he must depart, but his work will carry on, the damned leading the damned. And then He will come.

For now, there is still time to render a few more exes – and collect some of the little ones he's marked.

Who shall he begin with?

***

"Take me, dammit! Leave the kid alone!" Randy shouted, storming to the front of their cage and rattling the fence so hard that a section collapsed.

A dozen guns were on them, Randy raising his hands. "Take me," he said, this time with gathering resignation. "Please, he's just a kid."

Randy felt as if he were trying to reason with a rabid dog. The eyes behind the wolf mask gleamed with sinister intent as the man spun the chamber of a revolver.

"Fine," the man said. Some of the prisoners had started calling him Wolfman, but that was far too flippant a nickname for such a malignant cancer.

This man would kill them all, Randy feared, and he would thoroughly enjoy doing it.

***

Xeke grabbed Randy by the arm. "Don't do this. He wants me. Think about your kids."

Randy shoved him back. "*You're* a kid, for Christ's sake! Let me do this!"

Xeke couldn't watch, turning from the fences as the pistol was brought to Randy's head. The silence was like swallowed glass, and then came a metallic click, then another.

A few prisoners begged Wolfman to stop. Even some of the guards urged him to "think this through" and "just chill, man."

Virtually mindless with terror, one of the prisoners had gone to a very still, unblinking place. Others trembled and cried, flooded with hopelessness.

"We've got a lucky one, boys! This bastard survived two rounds of Roulette!" Wolfman shouted, then ordered Randy back to confinement. Xeke had wondered if Randy would try to swipe the gun, but there were too many of them. Even if you stole one gun or killed one guy, the others would finish you straight up.

"Who's next?" Wolfman hollered once Randy was imprisoned once more.

This time no one volunteered, their faces blanched with defeat. Xeke knew he would be chosen – the guy had wanted him the first time – and yet still he recoiled when Wolfman pointed at him.

"You're done, you little punk!" Wolfman's voice was muffled and monstrous behind the mask. "The bullet knows who it wants! The bullet always knows, sucker!"

"I'll go again," Randy said, but this time Wolfman refused.

"You've already had your turn, hero. Let the other scouts take their turn tying the knot."

"I said, I'll go again." There was mountainous firmness in Randy's voice, but it was useless in the little cage between the lockers.

"You try anything, and I'll shoot everyone, you hear?"

Randy stepped back from the fence. "It's okay," Xeke told him, forcing back tears. "It is what it is."

Everyone was begging and clamoring now, Xeke led out to the middle of the room by two men, his legs like spindles of crumbling clay, his head heavy and throbbing.

Wolfman grabbed him by the hair and let him squirm. "Ready to die, punk?"

Words of defiance bunched up in Xeke's throat, but he couldn't launch them, not this time. The panic was too much, his life like a frayed rope scraped along a jagged rock.

The muzzle nudged icily against his neck, then lifted to his forehead. Xeke detected cigarette breath whisking through the mask, extruded in waves of hatred.

There was a raw, agonizing protraction, Xeke's eyes clamping shut.

"Ready?" came Wolfman's whisper.

"Ready, sucker?"

"I can't hear you. Ready, motherfucker?"

Xeke held his breath. Clenched his fists. Heard blood pounding through his veins.

"Ready, shithead?"

But there was no click, no death blast, only a voice shouting, "Stop!"

Xeke stumbled free of Wolfman's grip and spun himself into collapse. Behind him, Wolfman challenged the intervener – the man in the lion mask from before.

"Who the fuck are you to stop me?" Wolfman demanded.

"I own you," the man said, his voice sharply familiar.

But before Xeke could confirm it, they were all blown backwards as if by hurricane force winds, Xeke jetted into the fences, Wolfman launched against the far wall, his mask knocked off to reveal a mad scientist's glare.

Dazed, Xeke looked up to find the lion's face looming over him. In a moment the mask was lifted, Dalton Rose kneeling beside him and taking his hand in a cryogenic grip. "You'll never guess what I saw tonight, Xeke." He shook his head. "I saw an angel become the Devil, that's what. Fucking scrambled, isn't it?"

Dalton's teeth were bloody but intact, all of them, skeins of red interlaced like the mouth of a dental patient who never flosses. Moreover, blood crusted from an X-shaped wound carved into Dalton's forehead.

"I thought we were friends, you fucking plunger. What did I ever do to you?" Dalton briefly surveyed the room, where almost everyone else seemed to be dead or unconscious from the blast. "You should have killed me, Xeke."

Dalton's eyes exceeded in color, almost glowing green-blue.

But how can his teeth be fixed? It's impossible.

For a moment the room was weirdly quiet, like one of those mid-flight spells where the other passengers' voices fade and all you hear is the hum of the engines.

Dalton gently leveled a hand against Xeke's forehead, then put the mask on again and stood. It wasn't until Dalton shouted, "See something, say something!", that Xeke realized the kid wasn't actually standing but instead hovering a few inches off the floor.

Xeke tried to pursue Dalton when he advanced toward the door, but a haze of exhaustion dragged him down, forced his eyes closed. It was like being anesthetized, one minute fading, the next minute gone.

Later, coming awake from a fogland of induced sleep, Xeke wondered if it had all been a nightmare.

Soon he would discover that everything had been shatteringly real.

BLAZE THE GRID

Chapter 7

Delivering food and supplies wherever they were needed, Harry crisscrossed the rows of cots in the gymnasium until he was dizzy from witnessing all of the blood and tears, pain and devastation, rage and confusion. The sounds of agony vibrated in his head, throbbed in his eardrums.

But everything had been normal when Harry dozed off that night. The local news had been uneventful, mostly a series of previews highlighting weekend sporting events and charity fundraisers.

Now Harry was at Tantasqua in the middle of the night, bustling through a makeshift hospital, doing whatever he could to help. An impressive amount of equipment had already been brought in, though not nearly enough to keep the badly wounded from sliding across the brink. Immersed in the madness, oblivious to how long he'd been there, Harry thought he saw the final flame of a gunshot man's life pinched out, stillness taking over his face, emptiness in his eyes.

It all seemed so important, Harry thought, remembering the early portions of the week, his mind retreating from the horrors. He'd raked diligently most of Monday and Tuesday evenings, carting off the last of the fallen leaves in a wheelbarrow as dusk slid peacefully into place. He'd graded exams and essays. He'd made lesson plans and plodded through homework assignments with unimaginably poor spelling – it got worse every year – but where were his students now?

Harry began to feel faint, close to dropping unconscious and finding himself on one of those cots. He tried not to look at the victims' faces anymore. He tried to tune out their screams and sobs and questions...*How do I get to Brimfield on side roads? Are any roads open? Have you seen the girl in this picture?*

Harry felt like a part of him crumbled away with each word, each story, each bit of hurt and fear. Their terror for separated loved ones mirrored his own, everyone drowning in the same helpless quag, no way to find out if family members were okay, no way to ascertain how far the attack had reached.

"We're at war," Harry murmured, then began to pray again.

***

Amie and her family occupied a circular table at the back of the cafeteria. The kitchen was crammed with volunteers. There'd recently been another delivery of food, someone had announced, and hot meals would be ready shortly.

The cafeteria smelled like most school cafeterias, a strange mix of oranges and Doritos. Amie was nibbling a banana, Jazzi taking little spoonfuls of apple sauce. The others ate lightly as well, a brisk silence hanging between them. Grandpa stared angrily down at the table as he ate, still incensed over being forced to give up his gun. Grammy kept fidgeting her fingers and taking deep breaths.

BLAZE THE GRID

"I heard a National Guard guy saying they have even bigger shelters set up at Smith and Wesson, Westover, and Mount Holyoke," Dad said. "They're mobilizing more troops, so it shouldn't be long."

"Until what?" Grandpa threw his hands up.

Dad bit into an apple. "Until they defeat whoever's doing this and restore order."

"We can only pray," Mom said.

Setting down her spoon, Jazzi said, "Can we all pray together? Sena and I always prayed, every night."

There was a momentary delay, then a joining of hands. But before a word of prayer could be offered, distant gunfire shredded the night anew.

"Stay here!" a soldier ordered, running for the doors. "Everyone stay here and stay down!"

Two cops and three Freedom Riders joined him, chaos rising down the hall. Amie felt a pair of arms clasp around her leg beneath the table, where Jazzi was shaking like a puppy in a thunderstorm, only the top portion of her beanie cap visible.

"It's okay, it's all right," Amie said reactively, incapable of further words.

***

Xeke awoke in a new place. Dimly lit, it was heaped with old desks and tables.

The last thing he remembered was Dalton…but had that really happened? The memories made Xeke stumble around and trip over his own questions, as well as the old furniture.

This can't be happening. It's not possible.

Unless there'd been a team of dental surgeons responding immediately and working without pause, there was no way Dalton could have had his teeth restored. And then there was the other horror Xeke had seen, the one that had left him septic.

A distant series of explosive sounds shuddered through the ceiling, followed by a torrent of screams. Xeke staggered through the narrow room, which wasn't a room at all but a sort of passageway, a thin door in the distance. It would surely be locked, Xeke held prisoner again, and all he'd wanted to do that night was go to Friendly's with his girlfriend.

The door was unlocked. Beyond it waited an expansive room inhabited solely by a massive wooden wheel equipped with chains and footholds. Hiding in the shadows like a predator, the wheel was attached to a rolling platform by thick columns. Above, somewhere up there in a darkened network of beams and trusses, came a slight buzzing noise.

Xeke stepped atavistically backward, as afraid of the wheel as a deer is of traffic, but the door swung shut behind him. This time it was locked.

BLAZE THE GRID

Chapter 8

Virgil mowed down a man who might have ended Steel's life, the first in a succession of kills as enemies poured from the pool hallway.

With a pair of pistols Virgil shot calmly and accurately, maneuvering as if he were in a training exercise, Steel at first reduced to an admiring spectator. But his own skills were soon on display again, an inexplicable calmness shining through him.

"Get down, Paul!" Steel shouted, but his friend was right there beside him, shooting and missing a man who ran at Virgil.

Steel, however, did not miss. In less than a minute their enemies were heaped before them, but Steel knew it was far from over.

He eyed the doors.

Paul spun to face the doors.

Tommy, Dominick, Bea, and her family – all huddled in a corner – turned as well.

It was as if an airhorn had blasted, everyone's gaze drawn to the front doors of Tantasqua High School. Yet the only sound had been a solitary tap against the glass.

Then came another.

And another.

There were faces out there, dozens of bloody faces and hands pressed against the doors. One of the hands, dragged downward, made a sickening smeary sound.

Grunting and groaning, the next wave of attackers began to gently sway like branches in a storm, perfectly rhythmic, right and then left, right and left. There was a dark collective gleam to their eyes that could make a bear turn and run.

"What the fuck are they doing?" one of the Freedom Riders said.

A menacing silence ruled, everyone held rapt and waiting, their guns trained on the doors.

Virgil took a few steps toward the doors. "Hold your fire, people! Maybe they'll turn back."

Tommy took Bea's arm. They'd come to the lobby to search for family members, but now they were caught in the crosshairs.

"We should get out while we can," Tommy said. "There's too many of them."

Virgil turned to face the group. "If you don't have a firearm, get to the second floor now. Everyone else – be prepared to retreat on my command."

Steel shook his head, hating the idea of running. "We fight to the death!" he shouted, surprised by the support he received. "We'll kill anyone else who comes at us!"

BLAZE THE GRID

"We only have so much firepower," Virgil said. "Clearly the enemy has breached our perimeter gates. There could be hundreds, possibly thousands, behind them. If we die, everyone in this school dies."

In haunting unison beyond the doors, the faces tilted – but Paul was more focused on the darkness. How could it possibly be night black out there?

This is really it. The end of civilization – the beginning of ruin.

"Steel, something massive is going on here, something unimaginable," Paul said, remembering the woods and what they'd encountered there…a sword with the word *Abandon* engraved in the hilt; a pocketknife; a noose; earlier, drawings illustrating profound doom.

Paul put a hand on his friend's shoulder. There was panicked desperation in Steel's eyes, the Freedom Riders having stepped up alongside him.

Beyond the doors, those bloody, watchful faces were still tilted. They had all stopped swaying and were now perfectly still, seemingly awaiting provocation.

"We should run!" someone shouted.

"Shoot them!" another man blurted.

Paul clutched Steel's shoulder. "We have a chance to leave, man. Let's get out of here before it's too late."

Steel shook his head. "I'm tired of running. It only leads to more running, an endless goddamn cycle. We fight."

There was no time for argument. Like a medieval army's pre-war ritual, the intruders began to stomp and rap the glass in sequences of three. Everything they did was synchronized, Paul heavy with dread, feeling as though they were standing downhill of an avalanche.

By then, the Sims brothers and Bea's family had almost made it to the east exit of the building – Dominick pushing Bea's father in his wheelchair – when they encountered a trio in robes and masks guarding the door.

For the others, the situation was yet another dose of insanity, but for Tommy, who'd seen one of the masks in a vision – the lion – the confrontation was a virtual death sentence, for he knew the rage of the boy behind the mask, no longer a boy but a monster.

"Who the hell are you people?" Dom said when the kid in the lion mask stepped forth.

A coarse, ancient voice strained out from the mask. "I am Death's son. I will make the perfect X."

At the front of the building, the doors shattered simultaneously, as if a tidal wave had caused them to explode in a musical burst.

Steel's knees twitched when the volume of attackers became apparent – hundreds of men rushing forth.

"Light 'em up!" Virgil shouted, Steel moving off to the side to shoot down attackers who skirted around the fusillade of three machine gunners.

The automatic gunfire suppressed all other sounds, a bone-vibrating cannonade. And yet many of their attackers did not fall, did not bleed, did not even decelerate. With outstretched, indestructible arms they came steadily forth, knocking guns away and shoving men down.

"Jesus Christ," Steel murmured, ducking as one of the attackers opened its mouth impossibly wide and snapped at him, its face gray and gaunt.

The machine gunners were quickly overwhelmed, screaming and collapsing as their faces were shredded, their guns firing into the ceiling and raining down sections of tile.

Steel jabbed one of the things in the eyes, green fluid squirting warmly, and only then did it fall. He kicked another one, elbowed a third, stiff-armed a fourth, wrangled a fifth to the floor, then whirled around and smashed yet another one down with a folding chair…but he knew he couldn't keep it up, not against this many attackers.

Steel turned, saw that most of the Freedom Riders and military people were fleeing, but the ground was slick with blood. A few men slipped and were devoured, three or four attackers leaping on each person's back, blood spurting in fountains from the victims' necks.

Steel dropped two more fiends, then leaped over several bodies in search of Paul. But he couldn't find his friend in the fleeing throng, his shouts useless against screams of suffering.

Paul had wanted to stay and help Steel, but a retreating Freedom Rider had grabbed his arm and shouted for him to run or die. Briefly motionless, Paul had dodged to the right just in time and taken the corridor leading to the cafeteria.

Some people were hiding in the caf, others spilling out into the hall.

None of them would get far.

Many of them would get killed.

***

"Follow me," the coarse voice instructed, and the mask was lifted to reveal a face Tommy had seen before…and suddenly Tommy knew his name, the elusive word finally snared.

"Dalton," he said flatly.

The boy's eyes widened, so much hate in those eyes.

"Don't do this," Tommy pleaded.

Shrugging, Dalton smiled emptily, mirthlessly, his turquoise eyes going a little glazed and windy…something shifting inside them? "It's already done."

BLAZE THE GRID

Chapter 9

The commercials had first appeared during Super Bowl 2023, a visceral series not designed to entertain but to provoke – to shake people free of habit and start them down a new path.

The path toward the grid.

The first commercial had featured Gary Orsillo, of Omaha, Nebraska. Walking along the shoulder of a gently undulating, two-lane twilight road, Gary had told the story of his son's death. There'd been a bad sun glare, Gary had explained, verging on tears. The pickup truck driver had been distracted by his phone, the vehicle drifting for just a few seconds. The driver hadn't even seen little Trevor Orsillo riding his bike in the shoulder.

Please, Gary had concluded, looking grimly into the camera, *let's all take this step to keep our children safe. We can't undo the past, but we owe it to our kids to shape the future.*

The commercial had faded hazily to black, DRIVERLESS.COM flashing at the center of the screen, leaving the Super Bowl commercial connoisseurs confused, for that ad hadn't been funny in the slightest. It hadn't even featured anyone famous, and no one had been drinking a Budweiser or eating chips.

Later, just before the halftime show, immediately preceding another winsome Coke ad, Colton Capps's story (Cleveland, OH) had marked the second commercial in the series. *New driverless breakthroughs will keep your family safe from people like me,* Capps had said with a severe expression, arms crossed, the camera zooming out to reveal a prison cell. *I was arrested for OUI six times, but they didn't put me away till the seventh one, when I killed a man and his pregnant wife.* Tears glistened in his eyes. *The road isn't safe, not with people like me out there.*

The third commercial, aired during quarter three, had offered a police officer's perspective, a Massachusetts state trooper assigned to the accident reconstruction team. She'd seen 571 fatal accidents in her career, most of them caused by distracted or impaired drivers. *Over 5,000 Americans are killed every year from distracted driving alone,* she'd informed.

The final commercial, aired immediately following the Q4 two-minute warning, had been shorter, featuring the creator himself, Providence Devlin, encircled by a group of little leaguers eating ice cream cones. *Together we can ensure that every trip is safe, that every parent comes home to his or her child after work, that no one ever gets that terrible phone call again. Together we can transcend,* he'd said. *Please visit* DRIVERLESS.COM *for more information. Why should we wait for our grandchildren to effect change when the responsibility lies entirely with us?*

The commercials, paid for by a coalition of insurance companies, had prodded millions toward the grid, but still much work had remained. It hadn't taken long, though, not with industry leaders and interest groups climbing aboard daily.

BLAZE THE GRID

Frank Alexander was the CEO of a Worcester, MA-based insurance company that had ascended from mediocrity to stardom with the passage of AVA. The staff had quadrupled and was still hiring. The company had moved its headquarters into a swanky downtown high-rise, "though not quite as high as our revenues," as Frank liked to boast.

Indeed, insurance was a good gig these days. Policyholders still had to keep buying in as a condition of vehicle ownership, but there were dramatically fewer payouts now, only when a grid dodger caused a wreck or an occasional fallen branch damaged a car. Otherwise Frank and his coworkers luxuriated in the grid. Frank's older cousin, Adam, on the contrary, hadn't enjoyed the effects of the grid. A personal injury attorney specializing in vehicle accidents, poor Adam's caseload had dried up like a summer stream since AVA took effect, just as Frank had predicted it would, hundreds of starving sharks after the same few fish.

But all of a sudden the sunshine was gone. The grid was down, toast, leveled, and it was fucking dark. Frank walked along the edge of Route 20, his hands still shaking. He felt like he was on drugs, a real bad trip. Smoke filled his lungs, buildings on fire all around him like a scene on CNN.

With the semi-auto pistol currently in his right hand, Frank had shot three people dead tonight. The first two men had threatened him, each demanding his money. The third man had only looked threatening to Frank, a black man running toward him on Highway 290 in Auburn, a hood pulled over his head.

He shouldn't have come at me so quick. None of them should have come at me. Goddamn Level Two Business Class – should have had a fucking manual option for the amount I paid! They left me stranded out here with the criminals.

Though his legs ached and burned, Frank forced himself to keep walking, one step west at a time toward home. He'd managed to run for several minutes on the highway, away from his disabled Mercedes, until finally he'd panted down the exit ramp from 290 and come to Route 12, sharp aches in his sides. Now, an hour later, he progressed along Route 20 West, a line of burning restaurants to his right, the Burger King as charbroiled as its patties.

Frank stopped rigidly, then ducked into hiding behind a half-filled picker bin. A group of people approached in the empty eastbound lanes, swearing and shouting like hoodlums, probably a bunch of minorities, Frank assumed. That meant they were carrying and could shoot far more accurately than Frank (it had taken him three shots to kill the last guy, the one who'd come too quickly at him on 290, rushing past a billboard reading: **WHO IS JESUS? CALL FOR TRUTH AT…**).

Frank sighed with relief when the hood rats moved on. He was sweating even with the cold wind constantly at him. His tie hung loosely around his neck, his shirt unbuttoned a quarter of the way down. And his hands refused to keep still, the gun seeming heavier with every mile.

BLAZE THE GRID

Ammunition was a growing concern. After he'd done the business tonight, there were only 29 rounds left…and still such a long way to go to reach Sturbridge, at least fifteen minutes by car, an unknowable number of people to kill in between.

Frank hated the sound of his own footsteps. It reinforced the knowledge that he was alone out here, no one to call for help because the phones were down, no one to give him a ride, certainly not those Freedom Riders bastards he kept hiding from whenever they rumbled by on their motorcycles. They'd been helping people on 290, but surely they were in on this somehow, the shitheads, a bunch of mercenaries one minute and faux-heroes the next, murder a familiar skill for most of them, the fucking war criminal imperialists.

"The war's on again, isn't it, boys?"

Frank hated the wind even more than the clapping of his shoes against the pavement. It drowned other sounds, providing cover to scummers intending harm. Frank often checked over his shoulder; and whenever a distant hum of a motor caught his attention, he retreated to hiding.

There was no such thing as too careful, his wife and son depending on him to make it home.

Frank could only pray his family was unhurt, but Gene had been left with his grandmother for the night, and almost every structure Frank had seen for miles was burning. Each image of destruction left him feeling even more alone, every mile closer to home bringing less relief and more dread.

And more guilt.

That idiot, why did he come at me so fast? Why didn't he just give me some space?

Almost a mile farther, Frank hid from an approaching convoy, a dozen trucks included, most of them flatbeds transporting the crushed remains of vehicles. Frank was nearing the Oxford town line now, and how excruciatingly long the trek was by foot, Frank's days on the University of New Hampshire track and field team in the distant past.

Despite the knotted, throbbing mass of fear and confusion in his head, Frank vividly remembered those Super Bowl commercials from 2023, the ones touting what would eventually become the grid.

Look at it now. I knew it was a horrible idea, but it sure was profitable.

Frank shook his head, stuck with a nagging thought that this was what he deserved. He'd built a six-bedroom house because of the grid. He'd golfed with the governor because of the grid.

And now, thanks to the grid, his knees were aching under the weight of each step, his mode of transportation no greater than that of homeless people.

And his family might be dead.

BLAZE THE GRID

Chapter 10

The children didn't dare leave the classroom after another distant eruption of gunfire spewed screams high into the air, scattering them like volcanic ash throughout the school.

Most of the kids were hiding in a little den between the wall and the teacher's desk, one boy cowering and crying beneath the desk. Other kids remained on their cots, including Gene and the girl whose name he still did not know.

They kept telling each other that someone would come, Rock or Mikaela or someone else. Gene tried hard not to cry, even when he thought of the man. He had been like a villain from the movies, except this man was not confined to a screen. He was real, and he could fly. He could hurt you and kill you, just the thought of him making Gene feel as if he'd swallowed a jagged stone.

Where are they? Why don't they come back?

The shootings downstairs – what if they had killed Rock and Mikaela? What if they had killed every adult who could help? What if the kids were alone now, and what if the hooded man was searching room by room?

Gene's eyes drifted back to the door. He'd found masking tape in the teacher's drawer a while back and taped a poster over the window, but that had done nothing to diminish his fear. At least no one could see into the room now, but the kids couldn't see out and therefore didn't know what was waiting for them out there.

Occasionally Gene got a strong sense that the man was right there, his face inches from the door. He was probably licking his lips and grinning. He was probably readying the blade. Gene relived the pain. It came back to him in amplified bursts…sliced skin, screams, laughter.

Blood.

Gene's eyes strayed back to the far wall, catching sight of something he hadn't seen before on one of the desks. It was a stack of papers banded together, but how had he missed it before? He was almost positive those desks had been empty.

A light thud nudged the door, Gene's muscles tensing. The others hadn't seemed to notice it.

"Did you hear that?" Gene asked the little girl.

She shook her head.

A moment later the thud came again, slightly louder than before, as if someone were kicking the door.

"There!" Gene pointed to the door. "Did you hear it?"

She hadn't, Gene left frustrated and even more fearful. If he was the only kid who could hear these sounds, then surely their creator was coming for him and no one else.

BLAZE THE GRID

It's him! It has to be!

Ten seconds passed. Twenty. Half a minute, but there were no further sounds.

Eventually Gene stood and went to the far wall. He pulled the rubber band off the stack of papers and flung it aside. They were all the same, at least a dozen booklets, the covers reading:

**Tantasqua High School Drama Department
presents
"The Divine Comedy: Inferno"**

Abandon all hope, ye who enter here

Gene didn't understand much of what was inside the booklets, many of the words too big. He flipped through to the last few pages – *CAST PROFILES* – where there were pictures above the words.

The first photo was of an older kid, probably in high school. He was smiling, and his hair was kind of long. **XEKE HAMILTON**, it said beside his photo, and below…*Cursed is he whose appetite for violence blackens his heart, his shade condemned to the wheel, where violence will blacken his every moment.*

Lower on the cast list was a black man: **PAUL SHANNON.** He looked nice, reminding Gene of his music teacher, Mr. Impemba, but the words said he was also cursed…*Cursed is he whose aspirations* *lift him too high, his shade condemned to eternal grounding, the clatter of the thief's wheels always at his back, perpetually threatening to steal his eyes so he can look no longer to the future.*

Gene scanned through a few other names and descriptions, all of them cursed for different reasons. The final photo belonged to **DALTON ROSE**. He looked sad and hurt, his features scrunched up the same way people's faces got after they ate a lemon...*Blessed is he who suffers and is beaten back by society, his shade destined to ascend and lord over all others...*

Gene tossed the booklet aside, wondering what a Divine Comedy might be. Nothing fun, that's for sure.

The thud came loudly this time, not once but a trio that startled all of the kids.

The door creaked partly open – *but it was locked, it was locked!* – darkness in the hallway beyond. Gene thought he saw something moving out there, but no one entered.

"Hello?" he called, his voice very small.

"Who's there?" the girl said.

No one answered. No one entered, the door creaking halfway open as if by the breath of a draft. Gene felt an urge to slam the door shut, but he couldn't even manage a step, his eyes fastened upon the door, his stomach tight and heavy.

BLAZE THE GRID

How did it open? It was locked!

Most of the kids were whimpering or whispering; only Gene, the little girl, and two other boys remained out in the open, perfectly still.

Finally Gene found the strength to move…but he felt like he would topple over. He took a few steps, his whole body going cold, the door seeming like it was a football field away. His teeth clicked relentlessly. A thin sweat clung to his face and arms.

He conquered another few steps, a gathering sense of responsibility outdueling his fears. He somehow knew no one else would close that door, and the man was not coming for them anyhow. He only wanted Gene, the boy with the X on his forehead. He'd said he would find Gene anywhere, and now the door was creaking another few inches to the bad side, nothing behind it but darkness.

He's out there, don't go, he's out there, and in his mind Gene could vividly see the man's bloody face. He could picture him hiding off to the side of the door, waiting. He could picture him wiping another kid's blood from his blade, grinning wolfishly. Only a little less frightening, he could picture the striped tiger mask worn by the crazy man who'd yelled at them to open the door and then disappeared.

Yet still Gene pressed on, hands held out in front of him, as if he were fumbling through a darkened room. Elsewhere in the building, the cacophony had wilted to lesser sounds. The gunfire had all but ceased.

Gene was almost to the door, a dry, involuntary swallow rattling down his throat. He looked back at the others, all eyes upon him.

"Hurry!" the little girl urged, and Gene ran, the classroom seeming to expand again.

When he finally reached the door, he thought he saw a hand extend from the darkness like a log poking up from black waters. It grasped for him, bony fingers curled.

Gene shoved the door shut but felt substantial resistance from the other side, like pushing a door shut against the wind. The air became very cool as Gene locked the door – then downright cold.

"You did it!" the girl cried, and the other kids offered words of praise and relief as well. One boy began to cry uncontrollably, the one who'd been hiding under the desk.

Gene glanced back at the door, half-expecting it to creep open again.

It remained shut and locked, the window still blocked by the poster Gene had taped over it with fear-inspired haste.

"We have to go," Gene decided, not even thinking it through, the words tumbling from his mouth.

His opposition was heavy, but the little girl agreed. "It's been too long," she said. "Rock and Mikaela should have been back by now."

BLAZE THE GRID

No one emerged from hiding. Even the two boys who'd been with them retreated behind the desk.

"We'll go alone then," the girl declared. "Come on," she said to Gene, and suddenly he wasn't so sure this was a good idea. It reminded him of that time last year when he'd devised a plan to transport himself to Old Orchard Beach, Maine, his family's yearly vacation spot. School had been about to start, summer dwindling like a sliver of sun destined to dive beyond the horizon hills, cool nights eager to caper in, and Gene hadn't been ready for new teachers and homework and getting up early. He'd loaded a few things into his red wagon and haphazardly coupled it to his bicycle with old leashes. Well rested, he'd been ready for a long ride.

Gene had barely made it out of the driveway on that cool, drizzly late August morning – a few snacks and articles of clothing in the wagon, a folded map he couldn't understand in his pocket – when his mother spotted him.

But now he really was venturing out on his own (well, not entirely alone – at least he had a friend with him as he pulled open the door and peered out into the darkened hallway).

"Ready?" she said.

He nodded, gulped, looked both ways as if he were on a street corner. He searched the nearly complete darkness, strained his eyes for movement. His fear had risen even higher, strong enough to produce dizziness. His pulse throbbed in his ears, making them ache.

They remained at the threshold a few moments longer, and then they committed irreversibly, like jumping off a diving board, no way to take it back when the girl closed the door behind them and they started walking.

Now the darkness was complete.

BLAZE THE GRID

Chapter 11

Amie's family didn't leave the cafeteria right away, the blasts of war exploding nearby, amplified by confinement. The gunfire was so heavy that it might as well have been coming from within the room.

A terrified silence ensued, and when the gunshots resumed again, Dad urged them to leave. "We can't wait any longer – they'll come here next!"

They hurried with a dozen others to the edge of the room. Through the windowed walls they could see more people fleeing down the hallway toward the west end of the school, though it wasn't nearly as heavy an exodus as before. Most of the previous occupants of the cafeteria, including the kitchen volunteers, had already departed with reckless panic, risking a path straight into the bullets.

Amie and the others might have done the same if Dad hadn't stopped them. But now they were forced to leave the cafeteria, sprinting down the hall away from the gunfire, veering right and approaching a set of double-doors.

The others who'd been in the cafeteria with them reached the doors first. "No!" a woman gasped. "They're locked! What do we do?"

One of the men was about to subject the doors to a kick, but from above rattled a clinking gate. It came down fast like a guillotine, separating them from the doors, the man jumping back just in time.

"Jesus Christ! What the hell is going on?" He shook the thin bars to no avail as another group of escapees arrived behind them.

"They've locked us in," a black man said, appearing beside Amie. "You see what's happening, don't you, day turning to night, order turning to chaos?"

"There has to be another way out!" Jazzi clung to Amie's leg like a life preserver, both arms wrapped tightly.

"There's no way out," came a giggling voice, and Amie's knees nearly failed when she saw him, suited and smiling twenty feet behind them down the hall, slowly drifting closer.

Dalton Rose offered Amie a sweeping wave. "Hey, Ames! Wanna blaze some people with me?"

His blue-green lagoon eyes were inscrutable, and not for the first time Amie found herself lost within them, the conveyor of memories taking her inexorably back, plopping her down in the seat of Dalton's uncle's Hellcat last May.

He was sexy in a somber, petulant way, Dalton Rose, his wavy brown hair carelessly flawless, his attitude like jagged glass when he was in school – but he could be funny at parties after a few drinks, his face so different when he smiled, bright and boyish. He could be very funny, in fact, and superbly strange with his stories, especially those surrounding his Leapland excursions and his encounter in an alley one day with a tattoo artist visiting from Bratislava, a man who'd allegedly worked frenny art on him.

Amie would never forget that hot, stormy May night with Dalton, a few drinks at a party convincing her to dodge the grid with him on Route 49, where patches of lightning flickered at the horizon. Amie screamed from terror and exhilaration when Dalton launched into a straightaway, bringing his uncle's old Hellcat up to 110 MPH, grid traffic parting for him like a biblical sea, vehicles in both directions defaulting to the breakdown lanes.

We apologize for this minor inconvenience, the Q voices would all be saying, motorists probably swearing and shouting. *Allowing passage of noncompliant vehicle. The authorities have been notified. Resuming sequence.*

The idea of committing such a serious crime would have been unthinkable for Amie on a normal night, but Dalton's defiance had ignited something deep inside her and made the burn endure. No longer did she want to go home. No longer did she fear the wrath of the drones and COMPLEX agents. A rapid, irrational trust had formed, and now she wanted to do it again!

"Who runs the grid, Ames? Blaze that shit all night!"

Vehicles were reduced to blurs of light after Dalton made a three-point turn and bulleted down the center of the road again, back through the same line of motorists they'd just stopped, heading south now, going far too fast for either of them to read the bright yellow **MANUAL VEHICLE OPERATION PROHIBITED** signs or glimpse the roadside cross near the town line, where a teenager had died a decade earlier from a street race wreck.

120 MPH…130…140…

For a breathlessly frightening yet electrifying brevity, Amie felt like they were flying. Engine blasting, the car seemed to not merely own the road but shred it, every acceleration pinning her against the seat. This was undeniably the most heart-plummeting rush she'd ever experienced.

And then it was over.

Dalton brought the car down to normal speed and yanked it onto a side road, Amie disappointed by the deceleration, like a girl who's just gotten off a roller coaster after an hour's wait.

"Done already?" she said, grabbing his arm, stunned to be craving more. COMPLEX would be hot for them now, but there was still time for another blaze.

"I'm never done," Dalton grinned, filling Amie with a heated rush that made her feel half-sick and yet wanting to kiss him at the same time. Other boys concocted wild stories of grid dodging – but for Dalton it was a triple-digit reality.

"We can go back another way if you want, just have to avoid the scanners," Dalton said. "I know where they all are – my uncle works for COMPLEX."

BLAZE THE GRID

"He does?"

"Yeah, and he's got a map of all the scanners in his files. He said more are going in soon – fucking COMPLEX bastards, scrambled as shit. They're planning to add hundreds of those ones that look like mailboxes, but I bet I could lose the drones."

"No, you couldn't," Amie said, remembering last night's news, the scanner drones tracking a grid dodger all the way to Portland, where the Maine COMPLEX agents were waiting for him.

"The Freedom Riders do it all the time," Dalton persisted.

"But they're in groups – the drones can only follow so many of them."

"True. You're right, I'd be screwed."

They came to a stop on a dark side road, traffic having resumed its normal flow back on Route 49 now that the grid dodgers had blown through. The engine rumbled, ready to blaze again, and the way Dalton had said it – *blaze* – something about the way he'd said it elicited a desperate need, molten and smoking. COMPLEX was surely closing in, but fuck it, no one could catch them tonight. Dalton couldn't be caught, it seemed; in a world where rules were king, Dalton did things his own way.

"How often do you come out here off grid?" Amie said, swept up in an almost mystic infatuation with this boy they called Rosey.

He shrugged. "A few times a week. The grid is so confining, you know? And life in general, it just…blows. I don't know, sometimes I get these urges to drive off one night and never come back, just leave it all behind and start somewhere new."

Amie's muscles weakened. She marveled at how perfectly he'd described that trapped, terry feeling.

Dalton pushed a hand through his hair and turned to Amie, his face limned beautifully in the red glow of the dashboard lights. Amie, caught and held in that strange vortex of magnetism, wanted him achingly in that moment, reminded of boy band posters and childhood crushes, Dalton's aura impeccably similar, like delicious looking candy you knew you could never have, not before dinner, not before bedtime, not ever. That kind of candy isn't good for you, her parents would say.

But now Amie could have him, maybe…if he wanted her, and it definitely seemed like he wanted her. She was alone in the darkness with Dalton Rose, and maybe she could have as much candy as she pleased…and as many stories about the Ink Man from Bratislava as she could tolerate. Maybe she'd even receive a whisper on the source of his scar.

Dalton slid his hand across to meet hers, their eyes drawn darkly together, time irrelevant, Amie's thoughts chaotic. She wondered if she heard a siren far, far off. She didn't care. The engine rumbled hungrily, drowning the distant oceanlike sweep of grid traffic.

BLAZE THE GRID

He's a psycho. He's hot. But he's an asshole. No, he's just misunderstood. What if he murders me? But he said I'm perfect – no one's ever told me that before.

No one even knows I'm out here.

He has great hair, though, and those eyes…I bet he's amazing…He drives really fast…Maybe he could blaze me, too. And he said I'm perfect.

He'll say anything to get laid.

I wonder how many girls he's been with.

Didn't someone say he had sex at 13?

I think I drank too much. I feel a little frenny.

Dalton clicked off the headlights, ushering in a deeper darkness. He leaned a little closer. They talked about meaningless yet somehow imperative things, every word opening a new door, Amie left lightheaded with a familiar urge, one that always led to regret. She shouldn't venture down this terrible track again tonight, she knew deeply and disgracefully. But here was a beautiful visitor at the door to her heart, bearing gifts of mystery and rebellion, and how could she send him away, especially now, when she was picturing Dalton Rose lounging poolside, sprawled across a deck chair in his swim shorts, tanned explicitly fine as now, with his hair in dampened tangles and shiny droplets clinging to the bronzed runnels that surely grooved along his midriff.

And what a picture that had so swiftly formed! It was as if the tip of a feather had been traced delicately along her thighs, but still the fear abounded.

Backward or forward? Nothing ventured, nothing gained, old people sometimes said.

He lives with his uncle. He moved here a few years ago. I wonder what happened to his parents.

Go home! Get out of here!

But I bet he's so much better than the others, and he wants me!

He only wants to boof. Run! Run now!

But Amie still wanted his danger, wanted to shatter the tranquil waters again because life was too short, deterioration and pain inescapable. It wouldn't always be this way, so young and alive. There was probably a hospital room or two waiting for her far down the road, and what if no boy as fine as Dalton ever wanted her again? The others could never compete with his looks, and at last Amie had found someone who understood her. She'd gleaned that much in less than an hour with him and his darkly enigmatic smirk. Dalton Rose understood what it felt like to look into the mirror and want to smash the glass with your skull. His comments a few moments ago proved that he knew how people could be suffocated by their own skin. He probably knew well the late-hour urges to self-destruct.

Undeniably, Amie shared almost the same wavelength with this boy who'd been a peripheral acquaintance before tonight.

Is this it? Is this what it's like to fall in love?

Amie assumed that Dalton's inner poison had something to do with his parents and why they weren't around. It had to be something terrible, but…

Can't waste this chance. It won't come again.

Her thoughts arrived in shrapnel shards of lust and fear. When the words finally dried up and lightning winked in the distance, there was only one thing left. They kissed.

Later, Dalton mixed a drink for her at his uncle's bar at the center of an otherwise empty house (a gravedigger, he called this concoction, rum and whiskey and lemon juice and, laughingly, some shitty-ass Coke). Then, kissing again, they drifted upstairs, the storm edging closer, the wind and rain coming a little stronger now. The lightning no longer flickered but flashed.

Gravedigger in hand, Amie found herself in Dalton's lap on his bedroom sofa, his skin lightly redolent with chlorine and cherries, the thin scar on his right cheek alluring, his hair with its own natural lift, it seemed, not a second of his time occupied by a blow-dryer…and his kiss was exquisitely vertiginous in its alternations, high and then low, lips to neck, fast and then slow, measured and unbridled – a combination that caused the room to lose its definition. Amie had heard the rumors, heard he was a plungelicker, and yet she wanted him furiously, the gravedigger starting to work on her, making her feel like she was back on the road with him, her surroundings reduced to a whirl of colors, his face the steady constant.

Briefly drawing back, Dalton reached into his shorts pocket and popped something into his mouth – and moments later he became strangely different, embarking on a paranoid rant about the evils of the grid. No longer did he stroke her hair or kiss her, consumed by an almost manic influence, the gentleness gone from his face, the sparkling calm gone from those bright lagoon eyes, replaced by something dark and eerie, particularly noticeable when the lightning menaced and his eyes lurched sidelong to the window, the curtains trembling as if someone stood behind them.

"She's…everywhere," Dalton murmured, his eyes wild and wary. "She'll never leave."

"What are you talking about?"

Ignoring the question, he pulled her close and kissed her again, Amie a little queasy now at the feel of him hard beneath his shorts. But with his kisses came a senseless redoubling impulse in her heart, hot and hungry, throbbing and mystifying in its wrongness, a fire with promises of chaos if she let it burn. It wouldn't be easily extinguished, though, not with Dalton's lips frenetically upon hers, his breath suffused with alcohol, the scents of cherries and chlorine lingering pleasantly beneath it.

Amie took his hands and brought him to a staggering stand.

He giggled. "I'm fucked up, Ames."

"What did you take?"

"It's really frenny shit. Want some? I swear it's cool."

"I...I don't think so."

She held him firm against his gathering dizziness. Whatever drugs he'd taken had cast a distant, searching sheen over his eyes, the dazed scramble of his expression awakening a dark desire in her heart and drawing it rapidly out.

Taken swiftly and absolutely by the drugs – coding himself to Leapland? – Dalton's kisses became ravaging, too much, Amie's enchantment broken. Now she was afraid of what he might do.

He's out of his mind. He isn't kissing me – he's probably kissing some LeapPorn girl. Get out of here!

Amie pulled back. She knew she had to get away from him. She couldn't possibly go further with him, but her hands fell to his shorts and yanked them down. There was a spell of flat disbelief, Amie's heart slamming with a percussive urge to strip him down and...what? She didn't know what she was doing, and for a reckless wreck of a moment, lifting his T-shirt and flinging it away, she wondered if she'd been drugged as well.

Something in the drink?

Dalton stumbled backward, onto the sofa, Amie coming atop him and taking it all in with distressed exhilaration: an odd scene of tattooed serpents and hellish creatures on his chest, the words FALLEN ANGEL stretching from shoulder to shoulder, his abs relentlessly toned, sculpted with the precision of a museum piece never to be deaccessioned. Even further down, where her fingers now traced – where the waistband of his contours met those delicious curves – the scents of cherries and chlorine were joined by that of aftershave.

Amie felt inundated, unsure where to start, as shivery as her first time – *Candy, fine, fine candy, explicitly the finest.* Dalton was just too much, delectable and catastrophic, and she hated herself for being arrested in this way…for peeling off the near diaphanous contours...for seizing what she had earlier imagined when she'd thought of him in the deck chair, fantasy becoming reality…for kissing him and taking him in her mouth and tasting him.

What am I doing? The drink! He must've put something in the drink!

Amie knew this was wrong, horrible. She wanted to undo it as Dalton's eyes fluttered shut in besieged bliss and he began to wince, but she couldn't stop herself. She had turned him into the passenger and she was accelerating fast, letting the velocity raise him nearly to the crowning capstone before abruptly letting off.

"Ready to blaze, Rosey-licious?" she giggled, stroking him lightly – and the darkness, her darkness, it was soaring all around them. Once a burgeoning shadow, the fully bloomed dark had spread rapidly outward and washed over her with singular, demented purpose; and she suddenly *had* to have him, no, no, not that simple – she had to hurt him, reduce him. The scales had been tipped the wrong way for some time now, this darkly dwelling force told her in a razor-edged epiphany, and now they needed to be balanced out, logical equilibrium, that's all, the same way a tilted picture must be straightened and a room can't be left half-vacuumed…

But Dalton had a darkness of his own, Amie surprised to feel a warm stickiness as his trembling hand closed around her arm. A little yelp escaped her when Dalton pulled himself up, his fingers dripping blood. A gleaming object fell from his hand – a razorblade – and a blendered smile spread across his lips.

He stumbled forward, contours clinging around an ankle, his face as maniacal as that of a jester, his scar glaring a little brighter.

"Hit me," he said in a faltering rasp, his eyes dilated and unfocused, as though he were searching for her in the dark. Amie was starting to think maybe he hadn't gone to Leapland but instead consumed some other hallucinogenic drug.

"Hit me, please!" He finished himself off in hot spurts against Amie's arm and bit down hard on his lip, drawing beads of blood. "Hit me, Amie, hit me!"

A strange menace of thunder clapped and died, without the typical rolling finish. Lightning careened through the room, and for a second Amie thought she saw faces pressed against the curtains, but no, of course not, just the drugs that were starting to have their way with *her* now as Dalton's strained breathing relaxed and he let out a spent exhalation, his fingertips bubbling up fresh blood.

Amie slapped his cheek, a sound like an oar rammed flat against water. "Did you drug me?"

"No, never."

She slapped him again, this time on the shoulder and with less intensity. For a while Dalton's face was plastic, inexpressive, and then another grin shined through. "Harder," he requested.

Jesus, he's insane! I have to get home, but how? No car!

It was as if she'd broomed down a massive wasp nest, and now, panicked, she was just starting to understand the consequences.

"Hit me, Amie! Cut me!"

"Dalton, what are you doing?" She took his uninjured hand, sticky though not from blood, and she suddenly felt entirely lucid and in control of herself again.

"I'm not D...Dalton." He grinned madly, searching, licking his bloody fingertips. "Amie, please, will you ch...chain me up outside and leave me?" He fumbled blindly for her and nearly fell, Amie restraining him and probably saving a hospital visit.

Poison candy, but don't you want to ride that rope swing he's got? came a thought jouncing through her horror.

Dalton latched onto her arm again, dragging a red trail down to her wrist. "P...please, Amie." He began to cry. "The chains are in the garage. I'll get them."

She turned, ran to the stairs, Dalton shouting at her, begging her to come back.

"I won't hurt you, I promise. Please don't leave me, Amie. I don't want to be alone."

He crawled through the doorway toward Amie as if gunshot, a burst of lightning painting him in even greater lunacy.

Amie pitied him, naked and pathetic, and it was like the curtain of Oz had been pulled back, Dalton Rose's inner chaos revealed. In school it was locked tightly away behind a sullen veneer, but now he was exposed before her, not merely stripped but shredded down to his core. Amie had hurriedly worked her way past the thorns to a place of acid and despair, where every last petal of the rose fell along with splashes of blood and tears.

A part of her wanted to hug Dalton, to tell him that everything would be okay, that she could get him some help…but what if things would never be okay for either of them? She knew how bad it hurt to hate yourself and what you've become and the feel beneath your own skin – the feel of being locked in a coffin. She knew these helpless feelings like the symptoms of a disease, symptoms perhaps to return for her tomorrow or next week or next month.

The disease always returned, and how badly had it ravaged Dalton? How far gone was he to cut himself and ask that she chain him up outside?

Get out! Get out now!

Amie barreled down the stairs, reached the front door, thunder shaking the walls, Dalton's shouts rising to screams when she stepped out into the gusting storm.

At the end of the driveway, soaked, she could faintly hear screams and clatters issuing from the big house. The rain was pounding down on her in wind-wrapped sheets, the Hellcat parked safely in the garage for the night, and Amie realized with panic that she'd forgotten her purse in the house. All of her valuables were inside it, among them her phone and shifter, but she couldn't go back, not with Dalton shouting and smashing things.

It took her over an hour to make it home, guided through the remnant rains by receding gasps of lightning, the thunder no longer audible after a while. It was frightening out there all alone on roads that felt more like horror movie nightscapes.

Stalking sounds occasionally rose above the abating winds, forcing her to look back into the storm dark – Footsteps down the road? Whispers in the woods? – but most frightening of all were the memories, Amie wondering almost the entire trip about the transmutations in Dalton and herself.

What happened to us? How did everything go so insane?

Amie took a long shower, the cold rainy soak taking a while to leave her bones (thank God her parents were away at her aunt's house for the weekend). Much later, she dreamed of a little boy crying in a hospital, broken and forgotten. The boy reached a small hand out to her, looking up at her from a bed, and Amie took his hand and whispered soothingly to him, gained his trust, wiped away his tears, only to coil a rope around his neck and secure his wrists in chains – and she proceeded to lash him and laugh at his suffering. Then she tossed him into the trunk of a car and asked if he wanted a Coke and – yes, please! – she made sure to shake it good and spray it in his face before slamming the lid shut.

When she awoke, the dream was buried deeply beneath others, unobtainable, long gone and faceless like the demons of night terrors. She felt rested but not renewed, mostly just sore.

The world was a smashed, lonely place – and far darker than she'd ever imagined.

Amie found Dalton on her porch that morning, the hood of his sweatshirt pulled tightly over his head as he often wore it, the index and middle fingers of his left hand bandaged at the tips. Eyes evasive, words minimal, he said he was sorry for last night and returned her things. She would later find gift cards to Panera Bread and Dairy Queen and Yankee Candle tucked inside her purse, but these strange attempts at apology only added to Dalton's pitiful state.

Caught in a daze, unable to think of anything to say to him as he shifted nervously on her porch and stared down at his feet, Amie was capable only of disturbed, reactive thoughts, among them: *I've seen him naked,* a thought whose foundation was literal, the rest toweringly figurative.

Dalton didn't speak to Amie again, didn't even nod at her in the hallways, just kept a distant gaze, and she could only imagine his shame. But here they were again, six months later, Dalton grinning at her. He held a mask at his side, and his eyes – something about them horrified her.

One of the men started forward, but Dalton held up a palm and the big man went skidding backward, bowling Grammy over.

Dalton's laughter was deranged. "Blazed you, motherfucker!" and he made a gun out of his fingers and blew it, winking at Amie before giving Grammy the middle finger.

"You're dead!" Dad hollered, rushing him with clenched fists.

Calmly, Dalton snapped the mask over his head, and what happened next Amie couldn't be sure.

BLAZE THE GRID

There was a surge of sun-bright, dazzling white that forced their eyes shut, and in the next moment they were seated in an auditorium, Jazzi crying, Dad murmuring in disbelief.

Amie's brain was momentarily empty but for the two words she'd discovered six months ago on Dalton's chest.

Chapter 12

The hot-white blaze had found them all, a bridge spanning time and space, culminating for each of them in the auditorium.

The green curtains were closed, a spotlight shining upon the stage (dim as a firefly in comparison to what they'd just endured).

Tommy tried to stand but felt a familiar helplessness, his muscles no longer in his control. Even his voice had been suppressed, his body completely numb. He could only stare straight ahead at the stage as a massive wooden wheel attached to a platform was rolled in from behind the curtains, masked men on either end, one pushing while the other tugged.

Tommy, in spite of his panicked paralysis, was able to recognize that he'd seen all of this somewhere before – in the middle, yes, it had been the scene of one of his nightmares, the wooden wheel especially memorable. Soon it would be used for the administration of pain and shame, like a Puritan pillory, and when the ten-foot high wheel was repositioned to face the seats, Tommy's eyes settled upon a teenager strapped down.

There's a way out. You know it, all you have to do is find it.

The image of a maze flashed into Tommy's head, dozens of little alleys and blockages and deceptions keeping him from the exit, only one true way out. Tommy was confident he'd been shown the escape route during his time in the middle, except he hadn't exactly been taking notes. It was like being driven somewhere blindfolded and trying to retrace the precise sequences.

The lion mask covering his face, Dalton pushed through the curtains and strode up to the wheel. His clothes were different than before, a black suit and vest.

Dalton spread his arms wide. "Ladies and louts, boys and bitches, welcome to Contrapasso, your personal journey through Hell!"

Seated in the second row, Tommy could see the shifting menace in Dalton's eyes. It was too late for him now, but the rest of them could still get out. Tommy just had to solve the maze.

Think! Come on, think!

The kid strapped to the wheel was sweating and grimacing. A head strap, along with restraints at his arms, legs, and chest, held him firmly in place.

***

Dalton laughed, cold and hollow as he looked up at Xeke. "How're you feeling, kid? Straps too tight? Should I loosen them for you a little?" He motioned as if to adjust the straps, then shrugged and said, "First you have to survive a round with the bees. Sound good?"

***

A hectic droning came from above, the swarm of bees like a black puff from a smokestack – and suddenly Tommy could move again. He jolted out of the seat, empowered not only by external gifts but also those working internally.

Two visions had just descended, but unless he could reach the girl whose face had most recently flashed across the screen of his mind, he knew these visions would be useless.

***

Xeke screamed when the bees came ravaging down at him, though for now they delayed employment of their stingers, instead circling Xeke in a carousel of torment.

Xeke begged Dalton to let him down, but all he could see was the bright stage and, beyond it, swaying shapes in a crowd of darkness.

"Please, Dalton! Let me go!"

"Did you let me go?" Dalton flashed him a triumphant grin, his eyes dark and different, something moving in them?

Indeed. Dalton's eyes were like the surface of an unknowably deep sea, something shifting within.

A moment later Dalton straightened convulsively, his head craning, his eyes fixing vacantly on Xeke. "Time to die," he whispered, an ancient and inhuman sound.

BLAZE THE GRID

***

Fully paralyzed, Amie was screaming inside, though not a sound escaped her. She brimmed with terror and hatred, everything bottled up and held down, ready to explode in a million shards all ticketed for Dalton Rose's throat.

Yet she knew Dalton wasn't willingly responsible. Something was controlling him, that much evident from what he'd done before. But what was it? And how was it able to control him?

Amie's tears had no outlet, unspilled and heavy against her eyelids. Watching the bees surround Xeke, she sobbed inwardly for her boyfriend, her head heavy with pressure. It made her feel as if she were floating, and then she realized she really was lifting, her muscles at least partially under her command again, her arms like ungraceful wings struggling to keep herself airborne.

Still she was rising, drifting dreamlike over the stage now, no one seeming to notice her. Panicked disbelief walloped her – *Too high, way too high!* – but she couldn't descend, not even when she stopped moving her arms.

Down below whirled an ocean of sound, the wheel beginning to rotate with soft groans. Amie's ears filled with airy echoes, like the wind cutting through a seashell. Almost to the ceiling, she was violently wrenched and twirled, feeling as though she were riding an inverted roller coaster, sometimes facing the floor, sometimes facing the darkened ceiling.

At last, impossibly, she landed upright on a catwalk, a man standing beside her. "It's all right," he whispered, holding his palms up. "Come with me. If we hurry, we can save them."

BLAZE THE GRID

Chapter 13

Harry Freed had known the country was headed in a bad direction. Since AVA's institution, people had no longer driven but *traveled.* Since the incorporation of Leapland, people had been even more detached from the world around them, their eyes ensnared by the happenings of hallucinations, and if you dared to disrupt them there would be a serious price to pay.

How badly had society crumbled, Harry had often wondered, to reach a point where people were required to haul their motorcycles and classic cars to driving parks and pay twenty bucks an hour to piddle around the course? What a truly pitiful sight it had been on the news, the poor blokes with their muscle cars, around and around they went like kids on a bloody go-kart course, confined to the track and constantly monitored.

Yes, the country had been careening toward a very bad place, but what was unfolding tonight was something entirely different, tragically transcendent, like a Nostradamus prediction lifted to the nth degree. It pumped the word *evil* with steroids and filled the world with metastasizing cancer. It burrowed deep and then sprang up in a new place, an unexpected place, the damage even worse than the previous attack.

This time, Harry wondered if it could get any worse. He couldn't bloody move, couldn't even bat an eyelash at the horrors spread out cruelly across the stage, a swarm of bees turned loose upon some poor kid fastened to a wooden wheel. They were assiduously converting Dante's harrowing journey into a 2030 remake – whoever *they* were.

Harry felt a shiver brush through him along with a presentiment that he would be hauled up to the stage next, except it wouldn't be the wheel waiting for him but something far worse.

At his periphery, Harry could see other victims staring straight ahead, paralyzed as well. Harry remembered the woods. Something had been there, watching him. Maybe it was present now, watching all of them, if not controlling them.

Harry tried to concentrate on his breathing, but he couldn't voluntarily inhale or exhale, each automatic breath bringing pain.

"It's time for the second circle!" the suited boy heralded with gleeful insanity.

Harry watched as a TV monitor was wheeled onto the stage…and then he was watching someone on the road, staggering diagonally toward the shoulder…

***

Paul not only awoke standing but in motion. The latest memory jittering around his head was that of a blinding white beam.

How did I get out here?

The road was empty. The sky was horizoned pink and orange, overspread with furrowed clouds. The colors were rich and baleful, as allusive of death as the Reaper's silhouette. Turning to face a night blue eastern sky, Paul half-expected a cluster of vultures to be encircling him.

It was then, facing east, that he heard it: a distant series of *clop-clups*, so thin as to be an auditory illusion – an extension of the cold wind. Though a fleeting sound, it endured long enough to send atavistic spasms of fear through Paul.

Clop-clup. Clop-clup. Clop-clup.

The sounds returned even louder and closer, then faded again. Paul squinted, searched the dark road. Empty.

It's only in your head.

Terror clawed at him as he stood there, searching and waiting, suddenly convinced of what he would eventually see – that which had first come for him at age seventeen, back when his life had been set on cruise control. He'd heard T.C. gaining on him that night he'd wound up at the Navy Pier, and now, decades later, The Curse was back, summoned by the Devil himself, called to ride the night road.

Trust God's plan. Trust that you'll see your family again.

They're dead, and soon you will be, too, came a daggering thought along the wind. Accompanying that thought were the sounds of hooves and wagon wheels, unmistakably loud.

Paul turned and began to run, certain that if he looked back now the stagecoach's lanterns would glare out of the distant eastern dark, a pair of predatory eyes fixed on the prey.

Paul's run became a sprint toward twilight, a sprint to keep hope and light alive. The wind gusted faster. To his right was a slanted sign:

**WEST
20**

To his left was a scanner, spray-painted with expletives and images. Up ahead, a large overhead sign advertised Countyline Driving Park, **Featuring the Only Max Speed Course in the State**.

With fatigue Paul began to slow considerably, his pounding footfalls muting whatever terrors might be bristling up behind him. The colors of twilight were already beginning to fade, diffusing to a paler pinkish-orange palette that spilled through the clouds. A thin scent of rain had snuck in, the wind flapping Paul's clothes.

He didn't even see the scattered pill bottles until he stumbled over one of them, white pills skittering out of the orange bottle. It was unlabeled, as were all the others, maybe fifty bottles stretching across the road.

Evil abounds. It wants me to give up.

Paul let his eyes flutter briefly shut. "With Your strength, I will stand resolute against this evil, Lord."

BLAZE THE GRID

At first his words felt hollow, as if he were one of those infomercial proselytizers who rattled on about salvation. Then, as the sounds rose up behind him again, his prayers were infused with a conviction that left him shaking.

He opened his eyes, slowly turned, saw the torchlights rounding a distant curve. His legs wobbled beneath him. His breaths were caught in his throat. He could even make out the stallions, dark forms emerging from lesser dark.

Indeed, The Curse was coming for him again. It was coming to take away his vision forever.

The driver's form towered above the stagecoach – the fullest dark of all, darker than the inside of a sunken chest – and the horses were cantering leisurely, barely expending an effort.

Paul felt a steep plummet in his chest, knowing the stallions would catch him. He would turn again and run, only to look back and find The Curse gaining quickly on him.

Nonetheless, Paul started into a new sprint, this one jolting pain through his knees. Coarse whispers called to him from the woods. Like a candle pinched out, the western colors were becoming gray and smoky, the clouds thickening.

Paul ran until he could go no longer, delirious with the burn of exhaustion and agony in his knees. The stagecoach was only five hundred feet back now, tendrils of gray-black mist marking every edge, as though it were a contraption of drizzling ink.

"They're coming, Paul!" echoed the whispers from the woods.

"They'll clamp your eyes open, Paul!"

"They'll show you the sunrise, Paul!"

Paul tried to angle into the woods, but he was barred by an invisible partition and forced to stay on the road. Ahead on the right was a colorful flashing sign marking the entrance to Countyline Driving Park, **Where Nostalgia is Born.**

Paul gritted through the pain, willing himself to reach the park, guided by an intuition that T.C. couldn't go in there. The instinct was amplified when Paul heard the cracking whip, the stallions chuffing into full speed. The wheels echoed wooden thunder, louder, louder, louder, T.C.'s shouts coming into clarity, the horses' hooves ascending to a waterfall roar.

Paul was almost there, so close, but the stallions tore down the space between them.

I won't make it! They're too fast!

The colorful sign beckoned, but cool black mist lashed out from the stagecoach and sank into Paul's flesh. He could feel the crawling dampness on his neck and in his hair, determined to slow him down, yet somehow he found a new gear, faster than his speed in high school.

The wind shellacked him, as though he were sticking his head out the window of a moving car.

BLAZE THE GRID

His arms came wheeling up at his sides like those of sprinters. The ground didn't even seem to thud beneath him anymore.

But behind him the lights were even brighter, and a sudden downpour soaked and slowed him.

The whip slammed repeatedly. The wheels and hooves roared like a stampede.

Paul, fifty feet from the entrance, risked a final backward glance, stunned to see the stagecoach upon him, T.C. reaching down with a vaporous arm as long as a baseball bat.

Paul dove toward the entrance, knowing he would fall short – but something brought him farther. He could feel it take hold of him and whisk him through the rain, then carry him within the partially opened park gates.

He came down lightly, the stagecoach rattling past and chasing down the departed sun, T.C. turning back with a featureless face of gushing black mist. Extending from the back of the stagecoach was a platform and a gleaming metal chair rigged with leather straps.

The rain abruptly stopped. Paul watched the coach clatter down the road, rising and dipping over little knolls, until finally the torches were just sparks on the gray horizon and the sounds were little more than vibrations in his head.

It's gone. I made it. I made it! Paul leaped high and kicked his heels together, pain awaiting his landing. *With Your wings I fly, Lord!*

The entry road stretched on emptily before him, glistening damply beneath streetlights. Drip-drops pattered down from trees, and the shallow puddles were hateful mirrors.

Dazed and exhausted, Paul limped down the road, his hands trembling. The wind had subsided and the whispers had been silenced, the night itself like a disappointed spectator.

Paul stopped rigidly. He thought he'd heard someone walking behind him, but the entry road was empty, the gates having closed.

Paul remembered the noose, the mass grave, the drawings, the sword. The memories carouseled mockingly, then slipped away into the darkness of the past.

Keep moving. You can't stop.

He drew in a deep breath and restarted, quickening his pace toward the entry booths, where people just hours earlier had checked in their classic cars and speedsters and cycles. These places were like miniature golf courses for driving, the options plentiful. You had your straight tracks for the guys who wanted to gun it; the scenic courses offered leisurely rides across covered bridges and around gentle bends; and there were even racetracks.

BLAZE THE GRID

They'd seemingly thought of everything when launching the grid.

Reaching the other side of the booths, Paul's eyes roamed across a sea of vehicles and trailers. The parking lot was as large as those of amusement parks – **UNLOADING LOT**, the signs read. Trailers stood with their gates open, the vehicles towing them having been shut down by the grid's failure. In their panicked haste, people had attempted to flee in their manual rides – the ones they'd brought on trailers – and apparently most of them had made it out.

Some of them hadn't. There had been a few crashes, one involving a lustrous red Chevy Nova, an ocean blue Ferrari, and a black Ford F-1 pickup (the Ferrari was the unanimous winner).

Paul pressed forward, weaving through an apocalypse parking lot worth millions, still wondering why he had been saved. Why bring him here? What was he supposed to find?

He kept expecting to come across someone. Surely they hadn't all left, but the place seemed deserted. At the end of the parking lot, five roads branched off at angles like outstretched fingers, signs guiding drivers to their roads of choice. Paul had always found it sad that you had to pay to drive. There was something insultingly gimmicky about the whole thing – *Take away their freedom and then charge them to have it back, but only hourly, then you have to pay up again. Or perhaps you can splurge for a day pass, but don't let the course officials catch you speeding unless you're on Max Speed One, the light forever green as long as you pay it to be.*

And what had it all come to when the owners of driving parks made millions? With a fleeting, half-maddened chuckle, Paul was glad the grid had collapsed on itself like a child's block tower stacked too high, hopefully never to return.

But when he stumbled over a pair of items, he was no longer chuckling. His eyes leaped and froze.

"No, it can't be. Impossible."

But somehow it was possible. In one hand Paul held the threadbare one-eyed pony he'd found in the house of drawings.

With the other hand he scooped up a second stuffed animal – a shredded teddy bear.

BLAZE THE GRID

Chapter 14

Dalton jumped and laughed and skipped around the wooden wheel, his power raging electrically and escaping through his fingertips. It felt like his first time all over again – like his hamstrings might burst through his flesh, like he might detonate into sparkles and confetti. He'd sliced his fingertips that night, painting his lips bloody as the gothmaestra with the black and red hair straddled him. He'd known with every droplet of pain that he was weak and needed to pay. He'd known that too much pain was never enough. He'd loved how that girl made him suffer.

Tonight he would make others suffer. The visions! He'd seen how they would suffer, especially his father, who'd gotten off easy, prison a waterside picnic beneath a tree in bloom compared to what Dalton would do to him. He would drive to Shirley and blaze anyone who dared to slow him down, and then the big hurt would arrive, harrow time, baby. Finally Dalton wouldn't have to bleed himself anymore, wouldn't have to deprive himself of meals, wouldn't have to look in the mirror and hate himself.

After everything you've suffered, you deserve this, Dalton had been told. *How much did you hate being struck down? How much would you love to never be struck down again?*

Dalton made a wide giddy circle around the wheel, feeling just as scrambled as he had that time in the puddled alley after the man from Bratislava inked and drugged him up. That Saturday had started with the Boy Scouts, of all things, Dalton's uncle forcing him to attend a meeting at the high school, where the smiley pervmaestro leader had talked about some dumbass toy car derby, said everyone was a winner for showing up. Dalton had promptly excused himself to the bathroom and proceeded to walk to the center of town to buy his first pack of leapers and pills from a lazy-eyed methlord. High as Everest, he'd muttered the rest of the day about how you didn't win by showing up – you got your ass slammed down and your face painted red by showing up, that's what. If you showed up early to help, you awoke with something new hurting – your arm, your knee, your face, your shoulder, your neck. If you showed up late, you got your bitch-ass sent cowering back to your bedroom, and don't you turn that fucking music up! Mom's dying down there and she needs you to go back downstairs and be a man, not a bitch. She needs you to shut the music off and save her, but you won't help, not even when she's begging you, not even in your dreams, too afraid to pull back the curtain and see your failure, your shame, your fucking weakness…but it was supposed to be a good Christmas this time.

More memories came whirling back to Dalton. The man from Bratislava had understood. He'd inked him up Rembrandt-like and frenny, told him pain was art's good price. Later, he'd laughed at Dalton's squishy pack of "baby leaps" and then provided Leapland coders to Autobahn – "the top dog" – and they'd blazed together, blaze and glory, Brati's hands dreamlike and misty upon Dalton's as they gripped the invisible wheel and blazed all of the fastest Euro cars. When it was done the man from Bratislava had held Dalton as he convulsed and puked – *Relax, first time's a motherfucking beetch* – and he'd said they would meet again one day, something about the army of the damned, something about being groomed for this all his life. Dalton had answered, yes, yes, yessy, absolutely, knowing that one fine day he would recognize the man – how could he miss him with the X gouged brightly into his forehead?

He found me when I was nothing. He kept his promise. Together we will own everyone.

***

Xeke was spun upside down and held there at length as Dalton laughed and taunted him.

"What do you say, Xeke, my awesome friend? Another spin?" He circled the wheel again. "I gotta check out for a bit, but you'll be in good hands till I get back."

Xeke's head was heavy and throbbing with the blood that had rushed to it. When the wheel was spun around to get him pointed upright again, he blinked hopelessly at the rows of faces staring back at him. The bees were gone; miraculously, Xeke had only been stung twice (both on the forehead), but now the repeated cycles of the wheel were delivering a new horror – that of attrition.

For a moment the auditorium was perfectly silent, and then came that brutal voice.

"Survivor of roulette!" the man shouted. "Survivor of the swarming wrath! But can he survive what comes next?"

Down below, the masked man capered into view. It was Wolfman, of course, tufts of gray hair jiggling out the back of the mask. He swooped around front of Xeke and faced the crowd. "Like what you see, folks? Don't worry – he's only at the second circle. You haven't seen nothing yet."

Silence. Empty faces. There were little kids out there, Xeke raised to even greater alarm at the sight of them.

"I'll view your collective silence as mesmerized joy." Wolfman gave the wheel a groaning spin, Xeke's nausea worsening. Now he was angled to his left; if he were a minute hand, his head would be pointed toward one o'clock.

Wolfman disappeared for a moment, and when he returned there was a bucket of gleaming metal in his hand. He selected one of the weapons – a golden, blue-finned dart.

"Bullseye," he whispered up at Xeke with simmering eyes.

***

Gene felt something cold shoved into his hand, and suddenly he could move. He could stand, too, but his voice remained lost somewhere very far away, so far that Gene feared he might never find it.

BLAZE THE GRID

He still couldn't remember how he'd gotten here. He'd been walking down the dark hallway with the girl…and then he'd woken up in this auditorium. Had he fallen asleep? No, he couldn't have, no way!

"Throw it when you're told," an old woman instructed Gene, nodding at the cold item she'd forced into his hand – a dart.

The woman's lips remained fixed and wooden when she spoke, her eyes lolling as if held loosely by springs. She moved on to the next row, put a dart in another kid's hand, said the same thing.

Gene, feeling suddenly as if he would pee, dropped the dart with a loud clink and ran for the side door. No one seemed to notice him as he went, and that got him moving even faster, rushing down an empty row as the man on stage addressed the crowd. But just as Gene was about to reach the side door, a tattooed man stood and blocked his path. He grabbed Gene's arm and restrained him, Gene pulling and twisting to get away, but the man was too strong, his eyes lolling just like the old woman.

The man's mouth came yawningly open to reveal a bed of stinking rusty nails for teeth. Gene knew he was about to be bitten, the man's breath hot upon his ear, yet suddenly the strength went out of his captor like a cut vine. His arms fell limply to his sides, his head sagging to his chest. A moment after his eyes fluttered shut, he crumpled heavily to the floor.

Gene turned and gasped with exultation when another man appeared. He leaped into Rock's arms.

***

Dazed, Amie allowed the man to lead her through a thin door from the catwalk to a loft storage room, where spare lights and rigging equipment were kept. It was musty and dimly lit, the man waving for Amie to follow him down the back staircase, each step agonizing – for it was another step further from Xeke.

"We can do this together. We can save Xeke," the man said, and Amie trusted him unquestioningly. There was something beyond explanation in his voice that gave Amie confidence.

At the base of the stairs they came to an empty hallway and slipped into the first classroom. It was then the man's features took shape; before he'd been essentially faceless to Amie, his mention of Xeke's name sufficient to make him an instant ally. Beneath a black fedora, the man's gray eyes matched his beard – and there was a hard-edged kindness to his face that inspired hope for Amie but also tears.

"How do you know Xeke?" she managed, but her attention was quickly diverted. "Jazzi!" she blurted, hearing the girl's voice from a side door leading to the next classroom.

Not only did Jazzi rush into Amie's embrace, but her parents and grandparents were close behind her. A few other people stepped inside as well, everyone keeping their voices low.

A stranger eventually came up to Amie, his face bright with recognition. "This is going to sound insane," he started, "but just hear me out, okay?"

On any other night the man's claims would have indeed sounded insane. But tonight Amie and her family listened, nodding with dire understanding as the man described what had come to him in visions.

"You're the most important piece," the man told Amie. "I think you can reach Dalton by mentioning his mother. I'm not sure how she died, but it was bad. It scarred him, filled him with hate. That's how they got to him – that's how they're controlling him."

Amie's eyes were so wide that she could feel a strained discomfort. She remembered that stormy night with Dalton and everything he'd done, and suddenly it all fit together – cutting himself with the razorblade; asking her to chain him up; that blendered smile stretching jaggedly across his lips.

Amie also remembered her own darkness from that night. It had surged up viciously with insane impulses to hurt and humiliate him. It had used her darkest hours and fed on them, processed them like an algorithm, and fit them into its own agenda.

"If I could have a moment, everyone. My name is Virgil Kalas – I'm with the Freedom Riders – well, maybe we should start calling ourselves the Freedom Fighters," the man who'd rescued Amie said in an elevated voice. He stood at the head of the room, joined by a copper who'd entered from the side as well. For the first time Amie noticed

Virgil's belt buckle cross, as well as a patch on his jacket that read:

FBI
Firm Believer In
JESUS

"Whatever we're up against," Virgil said, "we can defeat it if we all work together. There is a way."

His assurances were countered with terror.

"Those things aren't human!"

"Did you see what they did to those people?"

"That kid had us paralyzed! Were we drugged? It must have been drugs."

This latest comment had come from Amie's mother. Her grandparents were huddled together, repeatedly eyeing both doors. Jazzi stood at Amie's side, their hands drawn together.

Xeke will be okay. He'll make it, Amie thought, dimly aware that her positivity was only possible because of Jazzi's return.

"We'll talk more in a sec," the stranger whispered to Amie. "I'm Tommy, by the way."

"Amie," she said, forcing a smile.

"As everyone knows by now, we are dealing with forces beyond human limitations," Virgil continued, and the other voices faded to silence. "This evil can't be killed with guns alone. We have to reach deep within ourselves and find what God gave as our best defense. This is–"

"Somebody get me a gun already. I'll blow these bastards' heads off," Grandpa interrupted.

"Will you really, dusty?" came a laughing voice to Amie's left…and riding alongside her fear was a fleeting enchantment with Dalton Rose's smile.

She didn't know how long he'd been standing there, his eyes turbulent and in-between, neither here nor there, and somehow that was the most frightening part. Whatever was controlling him had bombed his soul and left it hollow.

Watching Dalton stagger forward with small steps, the mask in his hands, his hair slick with sweat, Amie was riddled by a self-loathing strong enough to make her feel as if she were sinking. She wished she could return to earlier years, long before she'd found herself lost in Dalton's riptide stare – but hadn't she wanted to stir the placid waters of her existence? Well, now she had, and the result was irrevocable, a cast stone that could never be recovered from the depths.

Dalton. He was looking only at Amie now, his eyes changed.

"Stay back!" Virgil warned. "Evil has no place in our hearts. In the name of Jesus Christ, I command you to release this kid!"

Still watching Amie, Dalton snapped the mask over his head. Jazzi was clinging to Amie's arm now, her parents stepping out in front of her – but Amie somehow knew none of it would do any good.

We can't win. We're gonna die.

Hot white light flooded forth. Amie's thoughts were drowned and then her consciousness. When she awoke, she was sitting upright in a car, a cold wind whipping her hair.

Movement. Light. It drizzled palely out ahead of her, bleak and gray as it spattered over the arrow-straight road. Glancing left to the driver's seat, Amie could see it for just a moment, the thing that controlled Dalton, enveloping him with shadowy appendages.

"I'm sorry, Amie," she thought she heard him say above the shrieking wind.

The road glowed silver beneath a full moon slipping through the clouds. Amie was in complete control of herself again, and she felt Dalton's hand brush against hers. Unmasked, he was driving fast down the tree-lined night road, blazing past senseless things...a horse-drawn carriage; a wheelchair moving of its own volition; and a slow-moving hearse, a cigarette tossed out the driver's window, bursting into sparks on the pavement.

"Where are we, Dalton? What's going on?"

"I always liked you, Amie." He smiled thinly in the shadow-dark, his eyes soft and searching. He obliged the road with a few casual glances, but mostly he was watching her.

Is it gone? Is it him again?

"Dalton, please, just let my family go," she blurted. "What is this? What's happening to you?"

Dalton shifted higher, the car responding with an easy acceleration. They were back in the Hellcat, Amie half-expecting lightning on the horizon.

I must be dreaming – but you don't question whether you're dreaming in a dream.

They ripped past a dump truck so fast that its headlights were just greenish glows in the mirror.

"Think we can blaze it up to two hundred?" Dalton grinned, speaking with the excitement of a little boy testing his new toy.

"Dalton, where are we going? Why did you take me away from my family?"

He was silent, a petulant scowl forming as he accelerated. Amie was pushed back against the seat, not merely by the speed but something unseen, a repelling force like that of two magnets' north poles pushed toward each other.

Suddenly Amie remembered what Tommy had told her about Dalton's mother, but she was afraid to ask the question right away, wondering if Dalton would veer off the road with surprise. She waited for him to round a curve and rush past a handful of vehicles;

one of them, Amie thought, was the same hearse they'd just passed.

When the road was empty again, she moved her mouth to work the words up, then gulped them back down. She searched Dalton's face, shadowed and dimly aglow with the hellish red dashboard lights.

"I don't know what it is about you," he said, glancing at her. "I just get this feeling, it's hard to explain, like I've known you forever." He let the car's speed fall, his hand reaching across for hers, but Amie pulled away.

"What happened to your mom, Dalton?"

She'd forced the words out, and it was as if a wall of ice had gone up between them, Amie sensing his pained astonishment radiate outward in a series of waves. She was unaware of the car's steady deceleration until she noticed that vehicles were now passing them.

Dalton eventually stopped in the middle of the lane, a stream of traffic going around them. Left arm draped over the steering wheel, he leaned forward in a daze.

"Tell me," she urged, touching his shoulder.

Dalton recoiled, jarring his elbow into the door, his eyes shining. It was just him now, nothing controlling him, Amie was sure of it. The line of vehicles having passed them, darkness enfolded the car like bat wings, and a heavy knowingness spread over Amie.

The evil would return for Dalton soon. There wasn't much time.

"That night we were together," Amie said, trying a new angle, "you said your name isn't Dalton." She took hold of his wrist, and this time he didn't resist, Amie's earlier hatred of him melting into a puddle of pity. The way he was sitting, angled toward her now, allowed the dashboard lights to accentuate the scar on his cheek…and the tears whispering down to meet it.

"It's a long story," he said, brushing away his tears. "We should go."

"No, not yet." Amie grabbed his hand and lifted it from the shifter. "Please, just talk to me. You've been torn up by this for years, holding it all inside." She squeezed his hand, cold and stiff. "You wanted to punish yourself that night. That's why you asked me to—"

"Just forget it!" He shoved open the door and stumbled onto the road, Amie scrambling out as well. When he turned to face her, the mask had found its place over his head once more.

"Take it off!" she begged. "They're controlling you with that thing, can't you see it? They're turning you into something you're not."

"How do you know what I am? You don't know anything about me!"

"You're right, I don't know you. No one knows you because you won't let anyone in. Your past is poisoning you, Dalton."

He undid the tie and flung it aside, then ripped open the top of the shirt, two buttons flying. "I'm gonna make it right. I will, you watch." His words were muffled beneath the mask, his eyes submerged in the darkness.

He started toward the car, but Amie stood in his way and pulled him into her. Raising an arm to yank the mask off, she thought she saw the teeth stretch into a snarl as it fell to the pavement, though there wasn't enough light spilling down from the moon to be sure.

Dalton's mouth was fixed in a strange rictus. A tuft of hair fell lazily across his forehead. His eyes whirled like coins down a funnel, and Amie shook him forcibly, fearing that if she lost him back to the darkness again it would be forever.

Finally his eyes stilled, and he took her lightly by the shoulders. "We have to go," he said in a strained voice. "It's a long way to Shirley. I can't let him get away with what he did."

Chapter 15

Frank Alexander finally reached Sturbridge, killing a teenager to get there.

He should have given up the bike. I had a goddamn gun on him – why didn't he just give it up?

At least he's with whoever he was crying for.

Frank had found the kid wailing beside his electric motor scooter in the shoulder of Route 20. Frank had asked politely for the bike, even offering to pay for it. He'd said he needed to find his son...

He'd done everything right, but still the stupid kid had refused him, sniffling and coughing and shouting at Frank to leave him alone. Precious seconds had passed, Frank's desperation so heavy as to press its weight on his shoulders.

Gene's life is depending on you, goddamn it! This guy is just sitting here crying, wasting a perfectly good bike that you could use to get home.

Panicking, it had almost seemed as if Frank's arm had lifted on its own, the pistol aimed at its target independent of Frank's will. He'd felt disconnected from himself as he threatened the kid, telling him the bike wasn't worth his life. But when the kid had resisted his threats and shouted for help, Frank had shot him in the leg and hopped on the bike...but leaving the poor guy screaming and writhing in the road had seemed cruel.

So Frank had brought a prompt end to his suffering, then delivered a confirmation shot to the chest, cognizant even as he did so of the expended ammo.

I'm a father, and my son is all alone. He should have understood. He should have helped me.

It was getting very late. Buzzing through the ruined center of Sturbridge, Frank felt naked and watched, as if he were having one of those arcane nightmares that always seemed to end around four a.m. He droned along carefully, leaning forward, his eyes fixed on the road ahead. He'd gotten to Sturbridge fairly quickly after commandeering the bike, even with a few obstacles to maneuver around (the bike's top speed was eighty, though he hadn't pushed it quite that fast).

Trying to focus solely on the road, he again got that strange sensation of detachment, as if an external influence kept stepping in and briefly taking over.

I only did what I had to, what any father would do. Gene needs me.

Frank spotted a threatening looking group ahead on the left. They were gathered in a parking lot, illuminated by the headlights of their motorcycles. They wore bandanas and leather jackets, definitely the Freedom Riders, and Frank's muscles joined in a collective clench as he rode past them, knowing they could hunt him down if they wanted to.

They all have guns, those lunatics. They'll finish me.

BLAZE THE GRID

Frank checked the mirrors, anticipating the dreaded pursuit like a pre-grid speeding driver passing a trooper, except this time the citation would be paid for with his life.

But the Riders remained where they were, and now Frank was coming up on the darkened Blackington Building to his right, so old as to be an anachronism. To his left was the Millyard Marketplace, three stories of lighted windows revealing a frantic scene inside, the terror in people's eyes discernible all the way from the road.

Frank knew their expressions matched his own. His little boy was out there somewhere, most likely alone, wondering when his dad would find him.

Frank's heart took a plunge when he rounded a slight curve and saw a blockade at the intersection of Routes 20 and 148. Two eighteen-wheelers were parked perpendicularly, one blocking Route 20 and the other sealing off Route 148 South. Lined up ahead of the trucks, protected by concrete barriers in the middle of the intersection, were dozens of soldiers.

Slowing nearly to a stop, Frank glanced to his right and saw a pair of military tanks in the brightly lit parking lot of Mandy's Dance Studio. On the rooftop of the building, two snipers were little more than crouching shadows, yet somehow Frank could make them out.

Like spiders creeping down from intricate gossamers, two soldiers avoided notice until they appeared at Frank's sides and herded him in.

Insulated by shields and tactical gear, they quickly had Frank up and away from the bike, ushering him toward a row of office trailers set up behind the tanks.

"I'm Sergeant Steven Stallings, U.S. Army," a wiry middle-aged man said once Frank was inside the first trailer. He wore thin glasses, his face incredibly taut, as if every muscle and blood vessel were stretched to its limit. Deep lines carved into his forehead, and he spoke with worried immediacy.

"The Tantasqua shelter has reached capacity and can't accept new residents," Sgt. Stallings said, handing Frank a bottle of water from the refrigerator. "Do you have family in the area?"

Frank explained his situation, Stallings's face softening when he learned about Gene.

"Most of the houses in the area have been destroyed, but thousands made it to the shelter," Stallings informed. "If your son is at Tantasqua, we're going to find him for you, Mr.–"

Stallings's words were chopped away by gunfire that shook the trailer. Frank scrambled out to the parking lot and sprinted behind the tanks, away from a river of gunmen marching south down Route 148 toward the blockade.

Spurs of ice ground together in Frank's gut, his fear like a series of punches. The way these marchers were moving, slowly and perfectly synchronized, lifted Frank to the zenith of terror. Their lockstep stomps shook the ground, producing a roar like that of machinery.

Frank remained crouched behind the tanks, knowing absolutely that if he was spotted he'd be killed. He couldn't see the marchers' faces from this distance, only their forms as they stomped past, rigid like Nazis, a seemingly endless line.

Frank tried to stay perfectly still, convinced that even a minor movement would betray him. When the train of humanity finally reached its end, a graveyard of soldiers was left in its wake, dozens splayed out in pools of blood. No one moved, the only sounds belonging to the fading stomps of a malignant procession.

What the fuck was that?

"I don't know, Frank," issued a crackly voice from the darkness. It sounded as if it had drifted brokenly from miles off, yet it also seemed to have risen energetically from within, hollow and windy.

Frank turned and ran north into the woods. The farther he got from the blockade, the blacker the woods became.

"Wrong way, Frank," came the voice again. This time the words whispered down from the trees.

Frank grabbed his weapon, searched up into the darkness of the nearest trees, then fired, positive he'd seen something scuttling across branches. He could feel its eyes on him, could feel its hatred spreading over him, strong enough to suffocate.

"Leave me alone or I'll blow your goddamn brain out!"

Frank ran trippingly and not far before he fell and slammed his shoulder into a tree, the gun skidding away. He ignored the pain – pain was nothing when there were footsteps behind him now, shuffling over autumn's dead leaves, advancing quickly.

Frank stood and jolted forward again, grabbing his gun and turning in search of the thing.

But he saw only trees shooting up from the darkness, a few drizzles of light seeping in from the distant blockade and nothing more. Then, like a face poking through theater curtains, he thought he saw the drapes of darkness briefly pulled apart to reveal the grinning countenance of the teenager he'd murdered.

"I have to get to my son!" Frank shoved a hand against his mouth.

It's all in your head. This night is making you crazy.

Frank kept moving, eventually angling closer to the road. He heard only his labored breaths.

Just keep going. Don't look back.

Frank came to the edge of the road and leaned against a scanner gantry. He didn't notice the car skulking darkly and quietly around a curve behind him, too preoccupied with his search for sidling movement. It wasn't until the tires snapped over a twig that Frank let out a yelp, for the vehicle was at his side – a black hearse.

Headlights clicked on a few moments after the driver stepped out. Affixed to the rear side of the vehicle, a landau bar gleamed as if by its own light source.

"Get in," the driver said with the stentorian voice of a storyteller. He was a middle-aged black man with sunglasses and a top hat, his trench coat flapping in the night wind.

With trembling fingers Frank jiggled his gun at the guy, feeling powerless even with a firearm…for what sort of psychosis could lead a man to smile so heartily with a gun pointed at him?

"I need to get home, and you're gonna take me, okay?" Frank gripped the gun in both hands now. "And if my house is destroyed, I'll need you to take me to Tantasqua."

The driver said nothing, only nodded, his hearse idling patiently. They were a long way from the lights of the blockade now, yet still the entire hearse shined enigmatically.

This is because of what you did. He knows what you did.

"Get in," the driver repeated, chuckling, and it was as if his laughter were the only sound in the world, seven continents and seas muted in deference to this man. "It is late, sir." The driver's coat flapped open in a cold gust, revealing the golden chain of a pocket watch. "We should be going now. Time waits for no man."

"Who are you? What are you doing out here?"

Chuckling again, the man brought a hand to his chin as if to ponder. "In consideration of the night's whims, I suppose you can call me Mr. Charon. A pleasure to meet you, sir, another traveler I've stumbled across on life's road. Each night is a new journey, and some wrong turns you can't ever make right." He pointed at Frank, his smile evaporating. "You're quite lost, mister – quite lost indeed."

Frank was nodding absently, the ghosts of his own creation tormenting him. He'd been remembering the first man just then, and how abruptly the life had flowed out of him in a gurgled mess.

Frank stepped – almost skated – forward. "Let's go," he conceded in a small voice, still pointing his gun even though he knew who was in control.

Smiling a little differently this time – triumphantly? – Charon rounded the hearse with the avidity of a boy on prom night and opened the door for his passenger. "The road awaits, mister."

The hearse was hot and smoky. An impeccable fiddle ushered Darius Rucker's "Wagon Wheel" over the radio. From the rearview mirror, three trinkets dangled at the edges of golden chains – the peace sign painted across a six-string; a silver ornament that read HOPE; and a lion's head.

BLAZE THE GRID

Run! Get out while you still can, but Frank waited dazedly as Charon came back around, the pistol briefly forgotten in his hands.

Smiling, Charon settled into the driver's seat and gripped the steering wheel. "Ah, at last a good tune. Radio sure ain't what it used to be, is it, mister?"

"How can you be driving? It's against the law." Frank's words were desperately otiose, his legs and back achy. When the car eased into motion, he became aware of a slight burn in his throat.

"I adhere only to the laws of the night, sir. Cigarette?" Charon asked in that deep, bubbly voice as he lit one for himself, its glowing tip like the nib of the Devil's pen, ready to write the next chapter of horror.

"I'll pass," Frank said, rubbing his now aching head. He tapped his gun to provide a semblance of control, then told the man his address.

Charon drove slowly and with both hands on the wheel. He'd donned a pair of black leather driving gloves, and every few minutes he tossed out a cigarette and replaced it from a seemingly endless supply within his coat, asking each time if Frank would like one.

They took a surprising turn to the east near the Mass. Pike overpass, Charon claiming that fires made Route 148 North impassable up ahead. Their next road was a thin, sinuous track through the woods. Burning houses beckoned brightly in the distance, and on the music played, from Sinatra to

B.B. King to Etta James, Charon merrily identifying each song and nodding along with the rhythms, sometimes drumming his gloved hands against the wheel.

With every burning house Frank envisioned his own home, Gene trapped inside, screaming for him. His head began to throb from the music, his throat desiccated.

"You sure this is the way?" Frank said after a while. He was perhaps ten minutes from home, but he'd never taken this road off 148 before.

"I navigate these parts in my sleep," Charon chuckled. "Been driving these roads for ages, it seems. Always a new passenger to find."

"What about your family? Why are you out here all alone?"

Silence. A long exhalation of smoke.

Frank wondered what drugs this guy might be on. They said there were new tranquilizers out, strong enough to calm a man as he crossed the border into North Korea with American flags piping out of his pack. Yet no amount of drugs could account for the sinister aura radiating hotly from the driver.

Make him stop. Get out now!

Up ahead, the woods on both sides of the road were on fire, smoke rolling like fog. Undisturbed, Charon tossed another cigarette out the window, except this time the night air didn't bring relief for Frank but instead propelled even more smoke into the car.

"Jesus, keep that window shut!" Frank snapped. "No more cigarettes, got it?"

Charon was eerily silent, his grin limned in firelight as they crept past another burning house. Two vehicles burned in the driveway, and a little shed burned out back. The trees were like birthday candles on a cake of black frosting, the entire area soon to be fully engulfed.

"Come on, can't you drive any faster?"

Crawling around a downhill curve, Charon stopped for a scared golden retriever darting one way and then the other, ultimately choosing to race off in the direction from which it had come.

"Poor, poor fellow," Charon remarked. "Not a night to be out there all alone."

With the windows rolled up tight again, the fires sounded like waterfalls eager to consume new victims. Relentless. Frank wanted to close his eyes to the disaster, but he knew what would find him in the darkness, the ghosts staggering out of their alcoves to harass him, especially the teenager who'd been crying with grief, his scooter at his side.

He only wanted to be left alone, and look what you did. You ended him, wasted him.

But he should have listened, damn it! I told him about my kid. He should have just given up the bike.

They came around another downward dip, approaching an odd-angled intersection where a rusted stop sign had fallen, no need to erect it after the grid had taken effect.

Even with smoke clotting heavily at the intersection, Frank spotted the street sign.

"Turn left!" he blurted, but Charon was already nosing gently in that direction, checking both ways three times before sliding out onto Upper Fiskdale Road.

It was then Frank heard the thud. Glancing for the first time into the darkened rear compartment of the hearse, his dilated eyes settled upon a shadow that was confirmed by the next patch of firelight as an oak casket. It was blanketed with a velvet brocade of red and gold, elaborate symbols neatly intertwined, Frank thinking he saw a few lion heads mixed in…but they were back in a dark stretch of road now, encountering a thick rush of smoke that forced Charon back into a crawl.

"Indeed, they've torn the land asunder with blades of fire."

"Just shut up and drive – we're almost there. In about a mile you're gonna see Lakeside Drive."

Silent, Charon puffed out a billow of smoke; he'd lit another cigarette, the bastard! Frank was about to yell at him again when he heard another thud.

A hot stab of fear went through him as he spun around. They were approaching a massive blaze that provided more than enough light to indicate a slight adjustment of the casket. It was pitched at a different angle now, no longer facing straight ahead on the aluminum deck but pointed a little toward Frank.

Back into darkness, where this time a double-thud jolted against the deck. When they reached the next fire, the casket had crept a few inches closer to Frank, the fabric having slid askew.

"Who do you have in there?" Frank demanded. "You kidnap someone?"

"You, sir, are my only passenger tonight," Charon answered, his ageless voice like ocean waves.

Grinning faintly, Charon rolled down the window and tossed out his cigarette.

"Hey!" Frank pointed his weapon, the snap of rage pulsing in his head. "What did I tell you, nigger? No more smokes! You might not take me seriously, but the last guy who ignored me – he's for the goddamn vultures now!"

Frank clutched at his stomach, wincing with a sharp pain. Charon kept on driving and grinning and smoking as additional thuds issued from the casket, each one accompanied by a creak, as if the lid were opening.

"Who do you have in there?" Frank shook the gun. "I'm not fucking around, buddy! Who's in there? I won't ask you again!"

Frank was answered only by the thudding casket, its lid now partly open, a shadowy, spidery hand poking through the five-inch gap.

"Who's in there, goddamn it?"

A shattering ring filled Frank's ears, Charon slumping into the steering wheel, the hearse easing to a stop without even leaving the lane. Frank pulled his gun away from Charon's head, then stumbled out of the vehicle with the pained panic of a swatted bee.

Stepping away from the hearse, Frank looked back with suffocating expectation, predicting Charon to be grinning at him, a new cigarette wedged between his lips.

But the man was still slumped against the wheel. Dead. Not a sound came from the rear compartment.

Starting into a painful run down the road, coughing on the smoky air, Frank repeatedly glanced back at the hearse, its headlights seeming each time to be a little closer than before.

But once Frank made it safely around a curve, both his fear and pain began to subside.

Swamplands surrounded the road, only a few distant pinches of orange in sight through the trees. And the darkness remained unbroken by headlights.

BLAZE THE GRID

Chapter 16

Raptor takes flight from the darkness, soaring toward the burgeoning blue of the farthest eastern skies, beyond which the window is closing.

Finally the armies are ready to sweep darkness over the land and seas. The ocean waves will be conquered by screams ricocheting from coast to coast and back again. The wind will convey each agony along, all these multitudes of delay invaluable because they allowed humanity to build its castles proudly. Now is the perfect time, for how can destruction triumph unless cities are allowed to rise? How can you take from them if nothing is given?

Now that the cities have risen to unimaginable heights, their collapses will be that much more crushing. The stripping away of hope will taste that much sweeter. The architecture of fear will transcend.

Raptor savors the view. Even from a great distance, he can see their terror mapped out along a cartogram of greater and lesser oranges. He can see his armies dominating.

The world is a theater of endless seats ready to be filled, the orchestra eager to display everything it has practiced, driverless technologies among its latest manipulations. Much earlier, the enemy gave mankind fire with which to cook meals and keep warm – and Raptor showed them how to burn villages and kill the ones they loathed. Over the centuries the enemy gave them weapons to defend their homes and families – and, ever so subtly, with a nudge no more significant than a gust of wind, Raptor showed them how to use those weapons to murder and take whatever they wanted. The enemy gave them religion and unity, of course – and Raptor showed them oppression and greed. The enemy gave them the gift of medicine – and Raptor showed them exploitation and overuse.

The enemy gave them strength – and Raptor came to them in times of greatest weakness.

For every utensil that can improve, assist, or strengthen, there are also applications for destruction – and with these latest technologies Raptor has bolstered his armies.

The masses don't yet comprehend the true meaning of destruction. Soon.

Very soon.

Chapter 17

Slouched on the floor against one of the student desks, Tommy awoke with a gasp. Like stones pushed up from the soil, more memories had come to him from the middle, but this time they had come after him as well, pursuing him down a darkened road.

The pterodactyl's wings had blazed thunder over the valley, pounding through the darkness behind Tommy. Once just a shadow silently crossing the moon, the thing had swooped steadily closer, its head resembling that of a snake. Glassy yellow eyes glowered out from scaly craters, and the wings were large enough to enfold twenty men.

Tommy had seen the thing in flashing bursts throughout his nightmare, the winged devil searching and scenting him out. The last thing he could remember was running into the woods, the menace unable to reach him there due to its size, shrieking with frustration from the moonlit sky and glaring down at him through the trees.

Tommy stood and made a little circle, confirming an absence of threats. He was exhausted, as if he'd been physically hauled back to the middle – and what was he to do with these latest visions?

The classroom was occupied by countless new faces. Bea, pale and drawn, was asleep at the back of the room. Her parents and some of the others were there as well, but where was Dominick?

We're all being controlled. They put us to sleep again.

Tommy ran to Bea and took her hand, waking her. "Bea, it's me, Tommy. Hey, have you seen my brother?"

She shook her head dazedly. "How did we get here? What's happening to us?"

"We're in Hell," her father murmured. There was a tired, twitching derangement in his eyes, the look of a man who has seen too much to process.

Tommy turned away from them, searching the packed room for the voice calling his name – a small, familiar voice – and then he saw the boy amidst the crowd, his forehead bandaged and smile beaming.

"Gene! Thank God you're okay!" Scooping up the boy, Tommy recognized the man standing beside him. "What's happening?" he asked Rock. "Is Virgil still here? How long were we all out?"

Rock pointed to the head of the classroom, where Virgil was talking emphatically to a man with long hair and a thick black beard. The ammo belt draped over the man's shoulders was long enough to create a strange resemblance to an Egyptian pharaoh, each golden jewel making promises of destruction. The guy was a walking arsenal, yet his weapons and ammo made Tommy feel less confident than frightened.

BLAZE THE GRID

Sweating with urgency, knowing there wasn't much time before the monster from his nightmares came ripping down through the night for real, Tommy left Gene with Rock and went to the front of the room.

"We have to get out of here right now," he told Virgil. "If we wait, we're all gonna die."

The man with the long hair and beard nodded. "That's what I've been saying. We can't sit here like ducks, gotta bring the fight to them." He pointed to the door. "Those things aren't invincible – I took down a few with my bare hands. And that piece of shit kid in the suit – I'll throw him off the fucking balcony!"

"Tommy, this is Sherman Steel Sparks," Virgil said, taking a few steps backward, as though Sherman were a psycho dog that might just lunge at you and snack on your arm.

Tommy hazarded a handshake, and with the meeting of flesh came another jolt from the middle. He'd seen something very briefly just then, Sherman walking on Route 49 with a man who'd appeared in an earlier vision. They'd all been traveling different stretches of road when the grid was deep-sixed, and now their roads had reached a collective junction, everyone brought together beneath one roof.

We all have to work together. We all have a purpose.

Tommy felt a little tug at his pant leg, Gene peering up at him with the eyes of a lost puppy.

Crouching, Tommy balled a fist and held it out for the boy, Gene at first unsure but then giving him a tepid bump.

"We'll get you back home soon, buddy. Do you still have that cross I gave you?"

He pulled it out from beneath his sweatshirt. "The man," he said, his expression darkening. "He'll come for me."

Steel, who'd been listening, took a knee to Gene's right and pointed to the rifles slung over his shoulder. "You stay with us, kid, and you'll be just fine."

Though a part of Tommy wanted to put some space – preferably a few miles – between himself and Steel, he didn't require visions to know the man would play a vital role in tonight's outcome. With such an impressive cache of weapons and ammunition, one thing was for certain: their fate wouldn't be blamed on running out of bullets.

While Tommy talked with the men up front, Dominick, Rock, Bea, and her family were having a discussion of their own. Dominick had just slipped free of sleep's grip, no one initially noticing him in the opposite corner.

"How can we trust this guy?" Bea's father said, side-eyeing Virgil. "Who's to say he isn't working with the enemy like Tim?"

BLAZE THE GRID

"We have to trust someone." Rock snapped a fresh magazine into his pistol and adjusted his Red Sox hat, the brim stained with age.

Dom nodded in the direction of his brother. "If we should be following anyone, it's Tommy."

"He's right," Bea said. "His visions could be our only chance."

Bea's mother shook her head. "We shouldn't waste time electing a leader – look what happened with Tim. We just need to survive until help comes."

Virgil was calling everyone to attention once more when Tommy nearly collapsed beneath the weight of a jarring vision. It was as if he'd previously been straining his eyes to see in a darkened room…and now the lights had been turned on to reveal the abject horrors of their enemy.

The vision proceeded rapidly, the winged fiend gliding in for a landing on a moonlit field – but when the beast struck the ground it sprouted legs and arms, its wings folding up like a tent. Tommy couldn't see much of the thing's face through the tall, swaying grass, only its searching yellow eyes.

This time, though, the beast was blind to Tommy standing one hundred feet away, obscured by a tree. It lifted its head and sniffed like a wolf, catching Tommy's scent after a while and leering in his direction.

Their eyes locked through the swaying grass. The beast started toward Tommy but then stopped, protracting his terror. Its head was tilted, its tongue smacking against scaly lips.

Tommy was slack-jawed with realization as Virgil rattled off a plan. They were the same, the man who'd hurt Gene and the demon who'd ruled the moonlit skies of Tommy's vision. In one form or another it was responsible for all of this, Tommy understood, and it hated him because he'd been given the miracle of foresight.

I can help stop it, but I need more visions. I need to know how to stop it.

Tommy glanced from one person to the next, almost sick with the need to protect them. He felt like the captain of a fully loaded ship, charged with safely transporting each soul across the blackest, fiercest sea.

"We can't make the world into something it's not," Virgil was saying, his voice calm. "At least not by ourselves. Individually we are nothing, but together there is strength…"

His words broke up, Tommy overwhelmed by the noise of his thoughts, a single word raining down through the chaos of his memories – the name of the ageless evil that poisoned the world in countless forms.

Its name was Raptor.

Chapter 18

Pulled along by the invisible rope of impulse, Paul navigated the Mustang around another series of S-curves. A pair of stuffed animals rode shotgun – the shredded teddy bear and the one-eyed pony. They'd been lying there together, seemingly waiting for Paul to come around and find them, but now he didn't know what to do with them.

Shortly after finding the little creatures, he'd discovered the rumbling Mustang a few hundred feet past the origin of *Scenic Course 1 – 3.5 mi.* Rather than drive back the way he'd come, toward the unloading lot and the entry road, instinct had impelled Paul forward. Now he was almost to the end of the course, a covered bridge up ahead.

"Waste of time," Paul laughed despairingly. "There's nothing for me here."

Squeezing the stuffed animals, wondering if he was slowly going insane, Paul let himself be transported back through the years. He could remember being a high school kid with a limitless future, his talents matched only by his ambition. He could hear his wife's laughter and his son's first words. He longed to see their faces, to look into their eyes, but what if they were already gone? What if all of these miles only led to more suffering?

"The car," he murmured, remembering.

The Mustang's license plate had read *GRDLCK*, but what significance was to be discovered in it?

The evil's just messing with me again, over and over. Day suddenly turning to night, the stagecoach, the damn stuffed animals – it's all just a series of torments. It wants to break me down and make me quit. It wants to steal every blessing.

Paul lurched out of the car and glanced skyward to the bright and indifferent stars. The brief storm clouds had long ago scattered, though the air was still redolent with rain.

"They keep tormenting me, Lord, but You give me strength. What is my purpose now?"

Only the wind replied, soughing coolly through the trees.

"I'm lost, my Lord. Please give me direction."

A series of clop-clups echoed directly behind Paul. With the whisper of a passing night ship, the stagecoach rolled up between Paul and the Mustang, its lanterns gliding mistily through the dark.

The coach came to a stop beside the car, swirls of black mist swarming as T.C. alighted with a sound like water dumped on a campfire. His face was amorphous, vapor piping out smokelike and swooping back to its master.

"Give your eyes to me, Paul," The Curse hissed. Its coat and hat were but tatters of mist.

Simply looking at T.C. caused Paul's vision to falter, the shadows and patches of dread-black that had marked his seventeenth year arresting him once more. He strained as his vision leaked away like water through cupped hands, but Maze's voice suddenly spurred him on, a source of inspiration that hadn't been there when T.C. first came to him in high school.

Soon Maze's voice was joined by Maddie's, and somehow Paul could see their faces, not as he'd envisioned them but how they really were, like looking at a photograph – and they were beautiful, his family. They were waiting for him, fearing for him.

"They're alive," Paul blurted, and that was all he needed, a flash of faith to light the darkness…but somehow T.C. knew he wouldn't be easily vanquished, for the mist funneled up into columns twenty feet high around Paul. Barbed black vines scuttled between the columns, interlacing to form a cage.

T.C. lashed his blurry whip against the pavement, crumbling it. "Give your eyes to me, Paul. If you refuse, I'll hold them open to dawn's first light!"

T.C.'s voice heightened to rival the crash of an angry tide against rocks, the vines climbing and knotting into an even thicker net of thorns. Though paralyzed with fear, Paul could still hear his wife's and son's voices. He could see their faces.

The hope they engendered sent Paul into a sprint through the enclosure, thorns tearing and burning him, T.C.'s whip cracking at him with bursts of lightning but missing.

Paul ran through the pain and hurdled over new assaults of springing vines. His foot hooked around one of them and blazed with an electric burn, strong enough to set his left sneaker on fire.

Landing hard on his shoulder, Paul kicked off the burning sneaker and ran for the car, which was now several yards off. Vines sprang up beneath the Mustang's tires. Black ropes of mist wrapped around the frame. Having escaped the immediate vicinity of T.C., Paul's vision began to improve. Now he could pick the road and trees out from the darkness, shadows becoming shapes again.

With shaky hands Paul freed his pistol and wasted a few unavailing bullets, which only allowed T.C. time to pull up the roots he'd put down and clamber back up to the coach's seat.

Fearing futility, Paul jerked open the driver's door and tumbled into the car, T.C.'s whip thundering to his left.

"Run him down!"

Shrieking, leaping back on their hind legs, the stallions shot forth as Paul hit the accelerator.

The Mustang raced up to sixty, but the Devil's horsepower kept pace, the black cloud rushing along with Paul like a tornado that has turned the tables on its chasers. Gouges of lightning knifed out against the Mustang's sides and windshield, the glass cracking.

BLAZE THE GRID

Paul tugged the car to the left, trying to ram T.C. off the road, but the mist rider offset the attempt with a countermove of equal strength. Black tendrils busted out the windows as the stagecoach veered behind Paul and swung to his right. With a shower of sparks and glass the two vehicles bounced off each other again and steadied.

"Damn you, motherfucker!"

Paul was about to swerve again when he noticed a sharp curve looming in the distance. A pair of yellow signs delivered salient warning, but neither the signs nor the massive trees hugging the road would induce even a hint of deceleration.

Closer to the curve, closer, its sharpness amplified by the voracious speed. Panic pressed at Paul as his vision declined again, his surroundings blurring.

Give your eyes to me, Paul!

In a desperate, enraged detonation, Paul's hatred for the Devil's mockery overflowed, producing a complete dismissal of fear that brought his foot down heavily on the accelerator. All his life he'd been assailed not simply by his disease, but also by its personification…pursuing him along Chicago streets, creeping down the darkened hallways of his childhood home, taunting him in nightmares. But no more. Whether he emerged victorious or deceased, Paul would be finished with the Devil and The Curse tonight.

The curve was fiercely upon him, the needle pegged at a blurry eighty. The extremity of his speed on such a sharp curve sent the car into a two-wheeling tilt, the coach leaning severely alongside the Mustang and then falling slightly behind. Together the vehicles defied physics, scraping and sparking against trees but somehow maintaining control.

As though someone else were driving, the Mustang remained partway off the pavement, shredding dirt and gravel, kissing bark, utilizing every last inch of drivable space around the curve.

Behind Paul, the stagecoach slewed like a toboggan on a frozen pond as it came out of the curve. In the rearview mirror Paul could see the lanterns veering violently back and forth, the stallions breaking free of their rig.

Paul, now a considerable distance ahead, brought the car almost to a stop after he witnessed an explosion in the mirror and felt vibrations tremor in his skull. Black smoke billowed thickly from the crash, as if a train of petroleum tank cars had derailed. In only a slightly smaller cloud of black, the unfettered stallions wailed and stormed past the Mustang, dissipating into the night.

Five hundred feet back, the flames expanded wildly and climbed the trees. For a moment Paul could only watch, unsure if it was all just a trick – yet another deception. There was even an urge to go back and check, to confirm that T.C. was dead.

Paul's vision, however, seemed to be the only confirmation he needed. It was vastly improved, allowing him to make out the words on a distant sign:

BLAZE THE GRID

Massachusetts Correctional Institute – Shirley
Commonwealth of Massachusetts

Paul looked in the mirror again, but this time only a dark road came into view – a different road. Gone was the flaming wreckage and the curve behind it. This was a straight road, Paul following it until he saw the lights of a sprawling prison complex ahead on the right.

He stopped the car, wondering whether God or the Devil had led him here.

The windows are fixed! And my sneaker, it's back on my foot! he realized, no longer even surprised by the night's impossibilities.

Paul slowly passed the prison – **MCI SHIRLEY** – its entrance blocked by DOC and National Guard vehicles. In the distance he saw a sign for Souza-Baranowski Correctional Center.

It was then he heard a single whispered word from the passenger seat – "Hot" – in what sounded like a child's voice.

Paul's eyes flashed to his right, but the only passengers were those two stuffed animals he'd found in the parking lot of Countyline Driving Park. Scooping them up with a maddened chuckle, he was ready to toss the toys out of the car when he noticed a leaf of paper peeking from the bear's stuffing.

The yellowed note had been addressed to him. After Paul read it he immediately made the sign of the cross and prayed, knowing what he must do but afraid he lacked the strength required of him.

BLAZE THE GRID

Chapter 19

Xeke was whirled around for perhaps the hundredth time. The worst agony was concentrated in his head, bottled up and boiling, as if every pint of blood had rushed there while he'd been suspended upside down. His face felt hot and bloated. His ears echoed with a whiny thrumming noise like a trapped fly. His eyes felt as if they would pop like olives left in a microwave, his vision clouded with mist and gray-yellow orbs that twinkled like fireflies.

Xeke's muscles ached from prolonged constraint. Spasms flickered through his neck and back, and his legs burned with cramps. With every revolution of the wheel, his skin was stretched and pinched by the restraints. His throat was desert dry. His screams hardly amounted to whispers, and the man in the wolf mask had circled and circled the entire time, rounding the wheel and curiously observing Xeke like a dog watching a treed squirrel, savoring the helplessness of his victim. Earlier, he'd hurled two knives at the wheel, one narrowly missing Xeke's shoulder, the other plunging into the wood just wide of his right ankle. Members of the audience had been forced to throw sharp objects at the wheel as well, everyone missing the mark.

Now Wolfman was stationary as he stared up at Xeke, his arms crossed and head tilted. "Does it hurt?"

With Xeke's blurred vision, the man was little more than a tall shape amidst the shadow-fog, like a silhouette behind a curtain. Xeke squeezed his eyes shut, yet still he wasn't free of those ludic orbs, which danced and flashed about his eyelids, indifferent to his suffering.

The pressure in his head and against his eyes made him think of cracked eggs and overinflated balloons and ruptured appendixes (his stomach felt taut and harrowed, though it didn't hurt nearly as bad as his head).

"What was that?" Wolfman took a few steps closer, and Xeke could suddenly see a few colors peeking through the fog. "I couldn't hear you, kid. You have to speak up. Big loud voice now – we want everyone in the audience to hear you. Otherwise it's no fun."

His laughter spat across the stage, Xeke wincing as a strong spasm curled into his neck and jolted down his spine. His head felt only marginally better now that he'd been right side up for a few minutes, allowing his other pains to creep to the forefront – like his chafed wrists and ankles from the restraints. When he'd been facing six o'clock, completely upside down, the entirety of his weight had been strained inversely by the straps/shackles like an amusement park ride from Hell.

"We'll have to keep him well hydrated, ladies and gentlemen," Wolfman said, then trotted out of view. A moment later he was climbing a ladder to Xeke's right, the sound of his voice steadily rising. "I've never done an intravenous drip before, but it should be easy enough."

Xeke bit down hard on his lip when the stinging jab poked into his right arm. He felt fresh tears in his eyes, and strangely he thought of Dalton and the torture he'd endured, most of his teeth broken or knocked out, his mouth like a horror movie makeup artist's masterpiece.

You deserve this for what you did to him.

Xeke knew the thought hadn't been his own. It was as if a ghoul had whispered into his ear.

Dalton. You deserve this for hurting him. You're the reason he's…different now.

As the IV line was snaked hurriedly into place, Xeke recalled dim memories from his fugue-like episode when he'd had Dalton at gunpoint. Having allowed hatred to take over, he'd sensed a nudge from behind and a guiding hand upon his own.

"This will keep him hydrated, folks," Wolfman announced, descending the ladder a short time later. "And my assistants will add a few hits of adrenaline in a minute. Don't want the little puke to pass out, not until the real fun starts." He clapped repeatedly. "Now for the grand finale. Who wants to help me cut him open? Come on, don't be shy – it'll be just like science class. Don't you want to see how biology works?"

Wolfman's shadow crossed in front of Xeke on the stage. "Come on, people. South of the wall they're embracing the experiments. It's all in the name of science."

Xeke's heart clouted painfully, to the point that a moment's fear conveyed the possibility of a heart attack. His inhalations were suddenly twisted and tattered with pain, as though his lungs had been dragged through rolls of barbwire.

"While we get everything ready," Wolfman said, "how about we make sure he's fully awake?"

Xeke's tongue shot out when the hot jolt exploded through his neck, the initial electric pain quickly downgrading to throbbing tingles. He could faintly detect the odor of something burning – roughly the same stench given off by those tennis racket bug zappers after you fry a moth.

Another jolt, then another one, progressing lower. "Where next, kid? Uh oh, is it time to wake up Mr. Winky? You ready for the big hurt?"

Xeke, mouth frothing, jeans damp, didn't even notice Wolfman fall from the ladder with a listless thud. There was another thud behind him, followed by a hoarse, sickly croak – but Xeke's world was consumed by agony.

Shadows fanned out around the wheel, unnoticed.

"It's all right, kid. We're gonna get you down."

Xeke's eyes rolled up at the sound of Virgil's voice, the air pushed out of him in a relieved exhalation.

Steel, who'd shot the masked men with a silencer-equipped pistol he'd acquired, covered the stage with his weapon. He was on a roll, and it reminded him very much of his days in the cage, except now his fists were augmented by firearms. Pretty much the same principles applied, though. You could always tell when the opponent was reeling. You could see it in his eyes and feel it in his weakened counterpunches, and when you knew he was declining it seemed to infuse strength into your own muscles. It made you quicker, sharper. You identified his wounds and exploited them. You made him overcompensate, you made him doubt himself, and ultimately you put him down.

Steel had exposed the weakness in the deaders, as he called them, and now everyone was targeting the stitched throats, Virgil and Rock combining to drop maybe fifty of them already. The men in masks had been much easier foes, as susceptible to bullets as sacks of shit.

Yet Steel knew the kid would be different, the punk with the lion mask whose power exceeded.

I'll use every last round if I have to, he thought, and permitted himself a smile.

Chapter 20

The others came awake slowly and dazedly, as if from hibernation. Harry Freed had been dreaming of the days when the Autonomous Vehicles Act became law. They had been almost Orwellian, those days, Homeland Security overseeing the three-year implementation phase of the grid. All new vehicles were required to adhere to AVA standards by 2028, Harry's dream taking him vividly back to the day he'd laughed at the government's stunning vehicle exchange proposals. Even junkers had been traded for brand new grid-compliant wheels.

This will save countless lives.

We must make sacrifices in the name of safety.

The price of refused transcendence is paid not with money but lives.

Harry blinked, wondering how long he'd been asleep. Then he remembered what happened previously, all of it, but there was no time to process it. People were stumbling about the auditorium and shouting and questioning, others running with guns in hand. They were like surgery patients collectively awakening on the bloody table, but there was no one around to answer any questions.

To Harry's left, an old woman hobbled into the auditorium, showing a handful of wallet-size pictures to anyone who would look, but she was knocked down by the fleeing frenzy. She desperately tried to gather up her photos, crawling and fumbling, Harry getting there just in time to help her up and recover all seven photos.

He guided the woman into a seat, her lips trembling and eventually releasing words. "Thank you, sir. Thank you very much." With shaking hands she neatened the photos into a little stack, and when she looked up at him again Harry felt like her teary blue eyes might melt him down to a puddle.

"You're a very kind man," she said, patting his arm. "I don't know what I'd do if I lost these photos. They're all I have left of my family."

"I'll help you find them," Harry blurted, not even realizing what he'd said until a little later, when he was sitting beside the woman and looking at the photos. Three of them showed children of varying ages, the rest adults. The old woman's name was Joan, and she told Harry that she'd been babysitting her youngest grandson that night.

"You'd never believe what happened. I keep wondering myself if it was all just a dream," she said. "But it couldn't have been – the pain was too real. I've never had such horrible pain in my life. I really was shot…right here," and she pointed to the junction of her neck and shoulder.

There were no visible wounds. For a few disbelieving moments Harry wondered if this woman had been maddened by the horrors she'd witnessed; or maybe her wound really had been made to disappear. Far stranger things were happening tonight, the greatest power wielded not by people with guns but instead those with masks, especially the teenager – a kid in a suit who on ordinary days would make the gals feel their temperatures rise when he smiled at them. Maybe they'd even swoon if he asked them to prom, a boy with that sort of face, but the dichotomy between outward and inward in his case was severe, almost literary in its irony, because on this night the boy's smile made you detect something sick and ugly festering inside him, as if hundreds of spiderlings had hatched in his heart and were skittering about.

Indeed, there was something very wrong with that young man. And the source of that wrongness allowed him to harness dark energies with the efficacy of a necromancer conjuring up spirits at a foggy midnight graveyard. You could see the darkness in his eyes, could hear it in his voice.

"It's going to be all right. We'll find your family," Harry said when Joan had exhausted herself of words, her face drawn and confused. She looked like a play actress who's forgotten her lines, improvisation eluding her altogether.

Joan put her arms lightly around him – arms frail enough to belong to a scarecrow. Even through her jacket Harry could feel her heart pounding as if to outdo the ticker Poe had invented beneath the rotten floorboards of the guilt-torn mind.

Harry patted her back, speechless himself now, and suddenly the woman exclaimed, "Frank! Frank!" She wrenched free of their embrace and hobbled into the aisle, trying to get someone's attention across the auditorium. "That's my son-in-law," she told Harry. "Frank! Frank, over here!"

At last the man with the pistol looked over at them (not that this description made him unique – everyone seemingly had a gun, some with multiple weapons). But this man was gripping his pistol a little differently than the others, and there was big trouble in his eyes.

"Where's Gene?" the man said when they came together, not even giving Joan a chance to reply before his rage thundered and he shook her by the shoulders. "Where is he, damn it? Where's my son?"

"Hey now, just calm down," Harry managed before the gun was shoved into his face.

"Stay out of this, old man! You want the next coffin? There's enough for everyone!"

Spittle surged from Frank's lips, his eyes animalistic with rage.

Harry, a little dizzy from the shock of Frank's threats, took a few steps backward. "Just calm down," he repeated, holding his hands up. "We'll find your son. Just–"

Harry didn't feel the pain, only the clap of gunfire rattling his eardrums and a hot burst of white light. He collapsed into a seat, the air belted out of him with a sound no more significant than that of a struck match. For a moment he saw the ensuing chaos, and then he was back in London, nighttime, The Eye brilliant in color in the distance. He was rocking gently, lying on his back with his head propped up, at first unaware of his immediate surroundings, then realizing he was on the Thames, Janey sitting at the head of the little rowboat, her silhouette backlit by a night blue sky. The splash of oars through the water was oddly peaceful, if not soporific.

Except it wasn't Janey, definitely not sweet Janey. His vision adjusting a little, Harry could see that it was a man up front, watching him.

Letting the oars still, the man grinned at Harry. He was a tall black man with a smile somehow more dazzling than the Millennium Wheel.

"W…where am I?" Harry tried to push himself up but couldn't move.

"Easy now. Just rest, lad," the man answered with a sonorous yet somehow gently susurrating voice. "We're almost across the river. Can you see her waiting for you on the other side?"

The shore was a dark place. Birds called from far off. The Wheel flashed and glittered.

"I don't see anyone."

The man nodded. "In time. Almost there now. Try to enjoy the view between the worlds – it's one very few shades wake in time to see."

With that the man returned to his unhurried rowing, the oars knocking rhythmically between the thole pins and delving down into the Thames. Checking the shore again, Harry thought for a second he saw a light spring up in the form of a woman.

BLAZE THE GRID

Chapter 21

Frank grabbed his mother-in-law's arm and dragged her out of the auditorium. His shot had ignited a powder keg to rival that of the pre-WWI Balkans. No one had been sure where the shot came from, and so they'd all started shooting at each other. It helped that another cluster of "sew jobs", as Frank had heard one man call them, had clunked into the auditorium just before he shot the old bastard.

It also helped that anyone carrying a gun could be accused – and that was almost everyone.

The world was a free-for-all of human and inhuman terrors – had been since the grid shut down – too insane to even describe as insane…but all Frank cared about was finding his son. Gene was close, so close, he sensed. If only it had been Gene to call out to Frank instead of Joan, who of course was here all by herself. She'd let him get away.

Joan yelped and bleated as Frank tore through the hallway. "Shut up," he snarled, pushing past gunmen who rushed into the auditorium. "You lost Gene, you useless bitch! Another word and I'll put a bullet in your head!"

There were more sew jobs in the lobby, listlessly streaming in from the breached front entrance like a river of toxic sludge. Frank angled left toward a staircase, where he threw Joan over his shoulder and took the stairs up to the second floor. It was quiet up here, the floor slippery with puddles of blood, Frank's shoes squeaking with excessive noise.

"Put me down, Frank! What's wrong with you?"

Exhausted, Frank shoved into the library and plopped his mother-in-law down amidst dozens of corpses, Joan screaming in pain and clutching her hip. At least fifty bodies were strewn about the library (more bodies than books, it seemed). Most of the victims' necks had been slashed, blood having ponded in wide haloes around them. Their eyes shined doll-like in death.

Frank cleared a few thousand bucks of technology off one of the tables, sat achingly down, and carefully counted his remaining rounds, grimacing when he confirmed the total. Only twenty rounds left; thank God for an extended mag, but that wasn't enough, not nearly enough.

Need more, way more, and he frantically searched the deceased, trying not to look into their eyes.

"Yes!" he said at last, grabbing a pistol from a man's belt. A few more of these and he would be back in business.

Joan, crawling in anguish, almost reached the circulation desk when Frank dragged her by the ankles to the center of the library. She was too afraid to scream, even when her face was slicked coolly with the blood of the dead. Pain radiated from her hip and daggered through her torso. Tears ventured silently down her cheeks. She felt like she would die from the pain alone.

"You know what, I never liked you very much," Frank said, putting his semi-auto on the table and leaving his acquisition belted for later.

"Frank, please, why are you doing this? We should be looking for Gene. We–"

"You had one job and you couldn't keep my kid safe!" he shouted, lifting the gun... *What's one more? Really, it's just one more death on a long night. She doesn't know where Gene is – she's fucking worthless!*

"I'm sorry, so sorry," she mewled. "I was shot, I swear, and Gene was gone when I woke up. What's wrong with you, Frank? Why are you doing this to me?"

"You weren't shot," he said quietly. "Don't you fucking lie to me. What really happened?"

"I don't know, I swear it! I was shot and I just...blacked out. When I came to, I was healed. Please, Frank, we should be looking for him. What are you doing?"

Finger on the trigger as he leveled the gun on her, Frank decided to rest a little longer, then figure out what to do with her.

Ten seconds later Frank decided resolutely that he couldn't endure the sight of her any longer and he shot his mother-in-law with surprising accuracy in the head.

A spurt of red mist. Joan fell flat onto her stomach, Frank keeping the gun on her for a while, jittery with anticipation – but she was deader than the grid.

"Finally you're quiet," he muttered, standing, wondering if he might be able to find a Coke somewhere. "Grid's down – anything goes."

He snuffled noisily like a drug addict. It had been a very long night and he could really use a Coke before he picked up the trail again for Gene.

Getting closer. So close.

A wounded middle-aged man stumbled into the library and asked Frank for help. "You gotta do something, man, I'm shot," he begged, clutching his bleeding shoulder.

Frank assisted him in leaving this world, then belted the man's pistol and departed the library with one less blubbering old woman over his shoulder and two more weapons in his belt.

Not a bad exchange.

If only I'd gone straight home after work and hadn't stopped at Danielle's house, he thought. *I would have gotten home in time. But Dani loves me, too.*

On his way back to the stairs, Frank saw a teenager stagger out of a classroom and limp toward him. He was unarmed, his chest bloody. He probably wasn't older than fifteen, and when he noticed Frank he stopped and held up his hands.

BLAZE THE GRID

"Please help me! I was stabbed!"

"It's all right, kid. I'll get you some help. Let me take a look."

Just as the fear vanished from the kid's face, replaced by incipient hope, Frank clapped the gun across his head and dropped him.

The kid fell face first with a sickening squish, Frank wishing he'd just shot him like all the others. But he couldn't waste another bullet, not with an entire town to perhaps kill in order to reach Gene.

It's every man for himself. That kid wouldn't have lasted long anyway.

Tired and lightheaded, checking the hall in both directions, Frank mumbled, "Where can I get a Coke in this goddamn place?"

Chapter 22

Tommy and Dominick sat beside each other in the back of the ambulance. They were accompanied by four National Guardsmen, a police officer named Randy Wilner, two Freedom Riders, and an ex-marine/weapons specialist named Vito Contreras. The Riders were up front, everyone else in back, sitting on three benches that formed a U in the compartment of the stripped down ambulance.

The vehicle had been repurposed into a doomsday prepper's dream, with bulletproof windows and a specialized alloy shield frame. Beneath Tommy and Dom, inside the benches, were enough weapons and ammunition to arm a group three times their size.

The plan was essentially a Hail Mary attempt, Virgil having dispatched the Sims brothers with a small group out of desperation.

"If we stay here and fight, chances are good we'll all be killed," Virgil had said with brutal honesty. "The best way you can help us is to keep following your visions and use the weapons God gave you. We can only pray He offers them quickly."

Though Virgil had only just met Tommy, he'd spoken with a strange knowingness, as if he'd been aware of the visions even before Tommy knew about them. There hadn't been a hint of the expected incredulity, even when Tommy had first described the visions, Virgil nodding comprehendingly and eventually assigning a group to accompany him.

Tommy had reluctantly parted with Bea and her family and Gene, who'd gone across the street to the junior high school with hundreds of others, guided by soldiers who'd recently arrived from the shelter at Westover Air Reserve Base. Now that the high school was susceptible to attackers, Virgil had ordered that everyone be moved to the junior high building.

But it was only a matter of time before the cancer spread, Tommy feared.

"Anything?" Dom asked, breaking the silence.

Tommy shook his head. "Not since we left."

As though Virgil were prophetic, a vision had come to Tommy immediately after they turned south out of the school. He'd seen a flash of a prison, given away solely by the rings of barbed wire. And he'd seen Dalton Rose's face, blood dripping from the X in his forehead, an X that came and went at evil's command…but it would always be carved into his heart.

The vision had died with Dalton's face, and the future had been blocked from Tommy's view ever since.

"What's the closest prison? Ludlow?" Vito said, looking up from the weapon he'd been preparing, a heavily accessorized submachine gun. "We should take a gamble and go there. It's a shot in the dark, but we can't wait much longer."

In a way, Tommy was thankful for the zombielike attackers. They underscored the supernatural involvement in the attack – and brought credence to Tommy's visions. Otherwise he probably would have been viewed as a religious zealot claiming he'd been lifted from a coma and given the gift of foresight to serve as God's hand in the war between good and evil. Surely these men wouldn't be here with him now unless they'd seen for themselves the imagination-defying depths of the enemy.

Tommy still couldn't shake the zombies' faces from his head, fish-scale gray and zippered with blood-crusted tracks, the stench of death surrounding them. The way they moved, rhythmical and dragging, left not a doubt as to the greater power of evil that was in control, mobilizing countless armies against humanity.

One of the zombies had come after Tommy as he left the school with the others, but Dom had shoved a hunting knife into its throat. When the thing had collapsed, Tommy saw something bulging at the throat zipper, crawly and clawed like a lobster, poking out through the spurting wound. Then the gray skin had muted to a softer color and the attacker's face had gone serene, his soul perhaps allowed to move on now that its prison had been destroyed.

Tommy bit down on his lip, hoping a little pain might elicit a vision. It didn't work, and now he was starting to panic, feeling an even greater responsibility than before. A group of people that could have defended the school had instead been sent out on a seemingly outlandish mission, driving aimlessly about until the lightning rod for visions finally drew in a bolt. Tommy still didn't understand. Why him? And why in this percolating manner? Why not all at once?

For a time he wondered if his visions were really coming from God, or if they were all just evil's lure. Perhaps they would run themselves into an ambush at the prison.

"Try not to force it. Just let it come nice and slow," Dom coached.

The others alternated between watching Tommy and talking amongst themselves. Closing his eyes, Tommy saw a flash of something, yellowish and dim, but too quickly it was gone.

There must be more. Why are they not coming to me?

"Turn off the lights," Tommy instructed, thinking desperately that darkness would help – and he felt exceeding relief when they switched off the dome lights. No longer did he feel like a caged animal surrounded by scientists with notepads, everyone scrutinizing him. Even when they hadn't been looking directly at him, their expectant glances had put pressure on him.

Tommy leaned back, closed his eyes, felt his muscles relax a little. He tried to conjure up a mental picture of the first chapter to chaos, when they'd come upon the black Mustang in the middle of Route 49, Tommy still confined to his wheelchair when he'd seen the letters, GRDLCK spelled out across the license plate.

He willed himself to see something new, but what came to him next was not a vision but a whisper from within. *Gridlock,* it said, then: *No escape.*

No escape from what?

There was no time to sort it out, for the whispered words formed an illogical train, Tommy feeling as if the darkness itself were speaking to him.

Pass the bill.

The price of refused transcendence is paid not with money but lives.

Distribute fear.

Build the wall.

It shall be called Operation Arch.

You will be rich in the new world.

Do not question. Just have a Coke.

You will be rich in the new world, just have a Coke.

Do not question, just have a Coke.

Build the wall, and have a Coke.

It is all in the name of safety.

BLAZE THE GRID

The Autonomous Vehicles Act saves lives.

Saves lives.

Saves lives.

Saves lives.

Just have a Coke.

Be the change.

And have a Coke.

Tommy covered his ears and let out a lengthy exhalation that silenced the oppressive words.

Closing his eyes once more, he saw only blackness. For a moment it seemed to waver a little, as though something might push through from another dimension – a word, an image, a face, anything.

But there was nothing, and all Tommy could do was pray.

Chapter 23

The wall is nearing completion. Through it the trains pass steadily, delivering countless lambs to their doom.

Up north, the battles rage on, Raptor's armies momentarily thwarted in some places by enemy forces. This does not enrage Raptor, not yet. Such a war would surely not be met with resignation from the onset, especially now that the enemy has involved itself. What troubles Raptor, however, is the elusiveness of the designated ones. It was not supposed to be this way – they were supposed to fall into absolute obedience. It is all or nothing. A cracked door is not a closed door. And shallow breaths only indicate that the heart still stubbornly beats.

Raptor will descend on the remaining insubordinates. They will be broken and converted to mindless leaders – and the conquest, regardless of the enemy's continued resistance, will be complete.

Chapter 24

Amie was quiet and calculating, unsure of the ever-changing percentages, Dalton at times seeming to command the majority of himself and at other times seeming to lose out to whatever had been driving him for most of these darkened miles.

Presently he was humming-singing behind the lion mask, replaying the same song over and over, Volbeat's "Heaven Nor Hell", he'd told her.

Amie considered jerking the wheel, but she kept holding out hope for a better resolution, as if the grid would restart itself and the cops would pull them over for noncompliant operation. What Amie would give to be arrested with Dalton for noncompliance – *All passengers shall likewise be arrested and charged,* the driverless operation certification handbook had read.

But the handbook was useless now. Laws no longer existed.

Dalton's "Heaven Nor Hell" lyrics resumed: "…I've heard that the Devil's walking around…"

Amie tried to tune him out. She thought of her family and Jazzi, tears springing as she stared ahead at the dark road.

"Almost there," Dalton finally said, his first words to her in twenty minutes. Then, in a childish singsong way, he added, "Dad's gonna di-ie. Dad's gonna di-ie." He tittered like a little girl ready for hopscotch. "I'm gonna blaze him, Ames, torture him explicitly. Like, cyclonically. Then I'm gonna put him in a trunk and let him rot. You can watch if you want. We'll get some Cokes and just chill afterward – it'll be so lit."

"You don't have to do this. Please don't do this, Dalton. You lost yourself – this isn't you."

He giggled wildly, choking on his own inhalations like a dog that has consumed too much water…and now Amie could hear it, something else breathing within him – a double respiration.

"Stupid hopeful girl," he said, this time in a different voice, deep and dark, the voice that might just reply to you sometime past midnight if you shout appealingly enough down a well and wait for the echoes to chase themselves off.

The voice froze Amie's flesh. It made her feel as if her bones were exposed.

Very slowly Dalton's gaze shifted from the road to Amie, silence like a wall between them, just her and the mask, his eyes impossible to see beyond it.

And what could possibly be said now? What could she say with her skin flayed away by fear and helplessness? What could she say now that *it* was watching her?

"The time is now," the voice said, Dalton's possessor no longer even glancing at the road but staring directly at Amie.

BLAZE THE GRID

Her fear reaching a drowning point, Amie tried to rip the mask off, wanting to see Dalton's face and confirm that some part of him was still there. But the mask wouldn't lift, wouldn't even move slightly, as if she were trying to strip him of his skin.

The mask felt different, too, warm and a little slick. Sweaty?

"Almost there," he said, and it was Dalton's voice again, the voice that had so flippantly spoken of committing federal offenses last May: *Let's blaze the grid, Ames, blaze all those dusters like pylons!*

Permafrost in her veins, Amie remained still and silent, if only to keep from hearing that other voice again. She would spend a lifetime in silence to spare herself from it…the voice of the midnight well, the voice behind the mask, the voice of the reflection that doesn't match your movements in the mirror, the voice of eternal pain.

The car came to an abrupt halt outside the entrance to a prison. But the place hadn't appeared in the distance and become steadily more defined; it had simply brightened into existence.

"What now tries to prevent?" Dalton murmured, staring ahead at the vehicles that blocked the road.

Two of them were prisoner transport vans, parked nose to nose.

Dalton lurched out of the car. "What now? What now? I'll blaze them, Ames. Watch me blaze them explicitly! I'll give them worse deaths than Shakespeare!"

He held up his hands, fingers extended to the sky as though he were a diviner. The ground began to shake, at first gently and then with the clatters of an earthquake.

Trees swayed and cracked. Branches collapsed. Birds fled.

The vans were compressed like crushed toys. On flattened tires they rolled clear of the road, Dalton controlling their movements with quick finger flicks. It looked as if he were swiping a shifter screen, and somehow Amie knew he was smiling behind the mask.

Two additional vehicles were removed with ease, but Dalton could not dispatch the man approaching from the woods across the street. The man moved cautiously, his arms lifted in an appeal for peace.

"Where are you going, Ames? Don't you wanna see me blaze this dude?"

Dalton wasn't even looking at her, still jabbing ineffectually at the air.

Amie tried to run, but an insurmountable rush of wind pushed her back, funneling her toward Dalton with the strength of a jet engine.

He grabbed her arm. "Watch me blaze him, Ames. I'm gonna cut him in half. I'm gonna" – he craned his neck upward, as if something had spoken down at him from the night sky – "yeah, sweet, perfect…I'm gonna take his eyes, Ames. Will you help me pull them out? It might be hard, but they want his eyes. We have to get his eyes."

Chapter 25

The prison guards did what Paul had repeatedly told them not to do. He'd warned them of what was coming and they'd forged a plan. This wasn't it.

Hidden behind trees in the woods across the street from the prison, the guards unleashed a fusillade at Dalton Rose. He was unaffected, of course, but the girl fell to the pavement in a cloud of red.

"Jesus, no!" Paul screamed, rushing toward Dalton and the girl, oblivious to the sounds of the guards launched airborne, their bodies shredded across the barbwire rolls atop the fences. Moments later their guns fell inside the fence line, one of them jigging on end and firing.

"Please, Lord, save her! Save this child!"

Kneeling at the girl's side, Paul felt temporary relief when she coughed and attempted to speak, her mouth fixed in a grimace. But before Paul could survey her injuries, he was spun around to face the lion mask.

"You don't want to do this, Dalton." Paul slowly stood. "Your mother doesn't want this for you, kid. She wants you to be happy. You deserve to be happy."

Wheezy inhalations came from within the mask, but there were no words.

Paul opened his jacket, offered the shredded bear and the note he'd found inside it. "This message is for you. Don't let this thing control you – don't let your hatred consume you."

There was a moment of darkly probing stillness and silence, followed by a scream that could shatter granite into dust. It blew Paul back ten feet and knocked him flat, and then the kid was on him, throttling him.

Paul tried to poke at Dalton's eyes through the warm, slimy slits in the mask, but his strength was flagging. The kid's eyes darkened, coal-black and smiling. The wind churned up angrily.

Sensing death a strand away, straining past the burn of overexertion from a supine position, Paul managed to wrench the mask loose. It wouldn't come off, though, countless fleshy skeins having cemented it to the kid's face.

Dalton cried out in pain and choked Paul even harder, but finally he ripped the mask free.

"Don't do this, kid!"

Paul's words came out as gibberish. Still he was pinned down, Dalton's grip crushing him with the strength of a vise. Paul clawed at the kid's arms, tried to jab at his eyes again, but there was no air left in his lungs and his vision was failing to shadows.

Just when Paul felt his final breath choking away and the world went white, Dalton released him. The kid was blinking dazedly, blood dripping from his forehead. He started toward the mask, but Paul grabbed his ankle and tripped him down.

Dalton jerked and kicked, but Paul somehow retained the strength to hold him. "Stay, just stay," he rasped. "This isn't you."

Dalton was dizzy and disoriented. The last thing he remembered was driving. Driving and hating.

But something in this man's eyes made the hate drain away.

"I'm sorry – for everything," Dalton said, and the man released him.

Kill Dad! Kill him now! Put on the mask!

The mask was spinning toplike fifteen feet away, rolling toward Dalton now, coming right up beside him, the eyes blinking blackly, the teeth grinning.

Kill Dad! And have a Coke when it's done. You're very thirsty.

Dalton could hear something swooping loudly overhead, but a new sound stole his attention: a girl's cries. Amie.

Amie! he remembered, standing, kicking the mask away when it knocked against his ankles.

Dalton rushed to Amie's side. "Amie, no! Oh my God, no!" He took off his jacket, lifted her head from the pavement, and slid the jacket in place as a pillow. He took her hand and told her she'd be okay, but her eyes fluttered shut, her face ashen with the creep of death. She'd been shot in the forearm and the chest, and, holding her, Dalton felt what he'd so violently resisted since his mother's death. He remembered blazing the grid with Amie and kissing her and wanting to be with her, but hate had ruined him as always.

Kill Dad! The thought was accompanied by an enduring roar from the mask, and with a desperate impulse Dalton ran for the lion's head.

"What are you doing?" The man lunged at Dalton, but he dodged around him.

He grabbed up the mask, put it on, resisted the thoughts it proffered. He flattened his palms against Amie's wounds, knowing it was impossible, but it was all he could do, just a flicker of hope – and he'd seen impossibilities made real tonight, the restoration of his teeth engendering his current idea.

He hated the feel of the mask conforming once more to him, darkness spreading through him. He knew he only had a few seconds before he would need to take off the mask again, not enough time, but still he pressed at Amie's wounds and willed them to heal.

He could hear music in his head now…*I saw an angel become the Devil…*

Paul at first would not allow himself to believe. Just a trick, another trick, it had to be, but where was the blood? And how was the girl standing under her own power?

From above came the wailing of birds, not the small ones but hawks, eagles – raptors.

Dalton held Amie's shoulders and quickly explained what Paul still couldn't believe to be true.

"I was shot?" Amie said, oblivious to the impending threat.

"Get in the car!" Paul shouted. He'd heard the aerial stampede before he'd seen it, a black rope snapping through the night.

They barely made it to the Mustang – which Paul had parked in the roadside grass – before hundreds of birds descended in a spear, crashing against the roof and splattering into the windshield, feathers and fluids streaking red-black. Dalton, the last to enter the vehicle, slammed the door just as a bird came tearing through, cutting it in half, blood spraying.

Amie was in the back with Dalton, and Paul strained to see the road beyond the smeared mess on the windshield. They were headed back the way Paul had come; he half-expected to reconvene with the Countyline Driving Park course, but instead he followed an unfamiliar road.

If only one of these roads would point him in the direction of Chicago.

Dalton was razored with adrenaline, shaking as though he'd come out of Leapland. He'd saved Amie…somehow, and his joy was matched only by his terrified disbelief. He reached for her hand and she leaned into him; he didn't want to look behind them, never wanted to look over his shoulder again.

The bird strike concluded with two final kamikazes that cracked the windshield.

"Damn you, bastards!" Paul kept his hands steady on the wheel, realizing when he braked hard around a curve just how fast he'd been going.

"Keep it on the road, boss," Dalton said. "If I'm gonna die tonight, I don't want it to be in a boring car crash."

They all shared an insane laugh at that, Paul wondering how he could possibly find laughter while evil poured over the world.

Five miles west they came upon a new disaster. A commercial airliner had crashed into a grocery store, only the flame-edged tail section visible from the road: Freedom West Airways. The fuselage and wings were consumed by an inferno that had spread to the vehicles in the parking lot and to the adjacent sporting goods store.

The road ahead, meanwhile, was clear. They hadn't passed a vehicle in either direction since leaving the prison.

"Do you think they took down the plane?" Amie said, breaking their stunned silence.

Dalton shrugged. "They're capable of anything."

Paul felt like a bomb had gone off and he was among the survivors staggering around and trying to find shelter.

"You're right about what you said earlier," Dalton told Paul. "The hate – it harrowed me. My past is a disease." Dalton didn't think he could go on, but the words spilled out and it felt good in a frenny, unburdening way, with Amie's hand in his.

The miles unfolded along with Dalton's story, Amie and Paul listening with a few interjections of sympathy.

"Every morning I wake up with hate," Dalton said after conveying his childhood trauma. "Drugs help, but you can't get high in your sleep. No matter what I take, I can't stop the nightmares."

After much wondering, the enigma of Dalton Rose had finally been revealed to Amie. It was much worse than she'd imagined, and now, knowing what he'd endured, she felt drawn to him in an illogical way that frightened her. The last hour felt like a dream, beginning when Dalton had told her about how he erased her gunshot wounds with his touch, converting the powers of evil to a healing capacity. Just thinking about it made Amie feel cold. Her wounds had vanished, Paul confirmed, though she couldn't even remember the pain.

She could recall what Dalton had done to Xeke back at the school, and it made her want to kill him. Yet she also found herself ready to forgive him for being overtaken by the evil. She'd seen its power throughout the night; she'd seen how it feasted on weakness and tormented those who combated it. And for a boy who'd been shattered by his father's sins and forced to grow up without parents, the road to evil had been paved with pain and hate.

Up front, Paul murmured, "What in God's name is that guy doing?"

Two hundred feet ahead, a black hearse was stretched sidelong across the road.

Chapter 26

"Turn on the light," Tommy said.

The darkness idea wasn't working, his visions having gone dry. He felt like a failure. This was a waste of men and resources.

Reaching into his pocket, he pulled out the little booklet Gene had given him before they'd parted ways. Reading the back, he saw Gene's **GOOD LUCK TOMMY** scrawled in black marker across the bottom, beneath columns of advertisements drawing people's attention to a pizza place, an overhead door company, an oil company, an antiques dealer, a Chinese restaurant, Countyline Driving Park, and Your Friends at the Sturbridge Senior Center.

Tommy's smile was thin and fleeting. He wondered if he would see the boy again.

"What's that?" Dom said.

"Gene gave it to me."

The others started to grumble as Tommy handed the booklet to Dom.

"We should get back to the school," one of them said.

"Yeah, this idea—"

"This is it!" Dom shouted, startling Tommy. "Jesus, it was right here all along!"

Dominick held the booklet open for Tommy, pointing to Dalton Rose's photo and an accompanying bio.

"'Blessed is he who suffers and is beaten back by society, his shade destined to ascend and lord over all others,'" Tommy read, carefully tracing his way along the lines, as if removing his finger from the page might cause the words to disappear. "'In time all oppressors will find themselves oppressed, the powerful to be crushed down and made powerless. It is the equilibrium of things, and it shall be found this night at Souza-Baranowski Correctional Center, when the cells of isolation find father and son reunited.'"

"That's gotta be it," Dom said. "That's the prison you saw. It must be, right?"

Tommy read the cover of the booklet:

**Tantasqua High School Drama Department presents
"The Divine Comedy: Inferno"**

Abandon all hope, ye who enter here

A look at the other faces in the **CAST PROFILES** section revealed a blurb about everyone presently in the van. Some were only one-liners, but no one had been given a positive forecast.

Tommy and Dominick were pictured beside each other: **THE BROTHERS SIMS**...*Cursed are they* *who dare to presume the false god has conferred upon them gifts of prophecy, their shades condemned to live forever blindfolded in reverse.*

Tommy was about to read Vito's profile when the van came to an abrupt stop. Like loose groceries they were bounced into each other, Tommy grabbing Dom's arm to prevent his brother from being tossed toward the front compartment.

"Watch the damn road!" Randy yelled, swiping his forehead and checking for blood.

The back end of the van was jolted up a few feet, as if someone had rigged it to a tow truck. Tommy and Dom held on to each other, everyone else joining hands as well, a few men bracing themselves against the walls.

"What the fuck is going on?" Vito demanded, but there was no reply from the driver or front passenger, who were hidden from view by a partition.

Tommy pointed to his left. Outside, the clink of chains rose up, and now the van was sliding slowly backward.

Randy managed to stand and edge his way toward the front compartment. "Talk to us, guys. What's happening?"

Their backward speed increased, throwing off Randy's balance. He teetered and fell to his knees, no one else daring to stand, the words from the booklet screaming back at Tommy.

BLAZE THE GRID

Boxed into the windowless back compartment, it was impossible to determine their speed. The original doors had been replaced with bulletproof steel doors designed to withstand heavy caliber fire, even explosives. The driver could view the perimeter of the vehicle by consulting a monitor split into quadrants featuring different camera angles, but in the back they were blinder than subway riders in a tunnel.

Crawling now, Randy slid open the door to the front compartment. "They're dead! Jesus Christ, someone slashed their throats!"

Green-faced and wobbly, Randy lurched as if to puke, then tried to stand but only got halfway up before a greater acceleration forced him down again – not only an increase of speed working against him but also the severity of angle. The pitch steepened to the point that Tommy was slanted into his brother.

When the van finally slowed and leveled off, its prisoners glanced at each other for a spell of exceeding terror. No one said a word, their eyes darting from one person to the next, each man expecting someone else to make a move.

It felt like the van had come to a stop, but Tommy wondered who would open the doors. Who would be the first to stick his neck out beneath the blade?

Tommy was the first to stand, but Randy and the others stepped past him, weapons ready. They shoved open the back doors and glared rifles into the darkness.

Tommy and Dom braced for the shred of gunfire. But there was only silence.

"How is this possible?" Randy finally said as they exited the van.

They were back in northern Sturbridge on Route 148, the lights of Tantasqua High School beaming in the distance. Shots echoed from the schoolgrounds, and Tommy thought he heard screams drifting along the wind.

"We were driving for at least ten minutes before the thing took over. How did it bring us back here so quick?" Dom stared up at the sky, tinges of indigo softening above the trees on the eastern horizon.

"Tonight, anything's possible," Tommy said.

"Amen to that." Randy kept his rifle on the dark woods, cranking it left and right at the sounds of snapped twigs. Something was in there, watching them, enjoying its dominion.

"We need to get to the junior high school," Tommy said. "Obviously whatever's doing this won't let us reach the prison."

One of the soldiers started walking north. "I'm done. Can't fight this shit. May God be with you boys."

"He's right," another soldier said before turning south. "Defending this place is a lost cause. We're in over our heads."

"Wait!" Tommy pleaded. "Without a big group, both schools will fall. The kids will die!"

"Everyone's already dying, man. We all better hide before we get our throats cut, too," a third soldier said, eyes bulging, and he jogged north to catch up to the first deserter, who'd already crossed the Brookfield line and was little more than a shadow receding into the night.

Eventually it was just Tommy, Dom, Randy and Vito left standing on the road between schools. Muzzle flashes sprayed through the high school windows, gunfire echoing off the striated predawn sky and thrumming in the pavement. Each rumbling bout made Tommy's bones shudder and his heart trampoline.

"What now?" Dom said, feeling like the enemy had backed them up to a precipice.

Tommy glanced to his right, where only a few lights from the junior high school peeked through the trees flanking the entry drive. "We need to defend that place with our lives – it's all we have left."

Randy nodded. "We'll build up the defenses throughout the school, maybe get some snipers on the roof." He turned to Vito. "We know where these things are weak, and we have to shut them down before they get close to the school. Once they're inside, it's game over."

Vito coughed and spat. "We've got more than enough ammo. The problem is finding people who can use it."

Chapter 27

Frank had almost reached the west exit of the high school when an old man hobbled through a door and stepped into his path.

Frank was about to mercy him – he'd taken to thinking of his kills as mercies, for he really was sparing these people from the horrible deaths they would have otherwise suffered – when the old man said his name.

"You've had quite the night, haven't you?" the powder-haired old fart said with a feeble squawk. There was an evil troll-like snicker to follow, and then he added, "Unfortunately, there aren't enough rounds in the world to kill them all. Only *we* possess the power to do that."

Frank drew back from the door and lowered his weapon, feeling powerless against the mystery of this man, just as he'd felt while riding with Charon. "What are you talking about? Who are you?"

From his brown overcoat the man produced a mask identical to one Frank had seen in the auditorium. A snarling wolf.

"Put it on," the old man encouraged, a wheedling glint creeping into his stare. "A man like you wants power, deserves power. All you have to do is put on the mask."

Frank tapped his pistol, then revealed the recent finds tucked into his belt. "I've got plenty of power, old loogie, believe me. Now what's the catch here? What aren't you telling me?"

The old man offered a salty, snagging grin and crossed his arms.

Mercy him and be done with it. You don't have time for this. Need a Coke. And then find Gene and kill the brothers.

Wait, what?

Frank stumbled over his own thoughts. This latest one scared him, made him feel like maybe all this mercying was starting to get to him. Combat fatigue, they'd once called it, right? And shell shock.

You'll get through it. You always do.

With a wink the old man tossed the mask to Frank.

"What is this? What are you doing?"

"Just put it on," the man urged calmly and coaxingly. "Take the power."

"I'll think about it," Frank conceded, taking an inexplicable liking to the mask now that it was in his hands. The way the teeth angled out into a bright snarl, the way the fur seemed to climb to hackles – the idea of wearing it warmed Frank with a frisson.

The old man was nodding now. "Take the power. You will put the world on its knees."

Frank pointed the gun. "I said I'll think about it. Now get out of my face!"

Slowly, still smirking, the old man receded as if pulled by an invisible rope.

"That's it, that's it," Frank said as the man backed through the door and disappeared.

Need a Coke. Could really use a goddamn Coke.

Deciding to keep the mask for now, Frank checked his ammo and then hurried outside; no sign of the old man. Jogging down the back walkway toward the loading docks, Frank came upon a pair of men in the shadows and mercied them without even aiming, his hands reacting reflexively.

When he reached the loading docks bathed in the orange glow of lamps, Frank crept behind a truck and took another inventory of his ammo. Then, unthinkingly, he put the mask over his head and let his eyes adjust to the world beyond the slits.

Need a Coke. Kill the brothers. What brothers? But suddenly he knew, and it was like he'd known all along. *Yes, of course. The Sims brothers must die, and then the grid must start again.*

Even though his eyes were now closed, Frank somehow knew infallibly that a man was coming at him from the left. Without opening his eyes, letting his arm guide the way, he lifted the pistol until it felt just right, perfectly balanced…and then he shot the man, his death gasp bringing Frank's eyes open.

BLAZE THE GRID

I'll mercy everyone who stands between me and my son. Every last one.

Frank managed to pull off the mask with an earnest tug, his fears quickly quelled.

It will all be fine, just fine. Just gotta get a Coke, that's all. The rest will fall into place from there.

He stared absently at the mask for a while, feeling nauseous without it.

Coke. Need a Coke.

Frank hastened the mask over his face again. He didn't bother recovering the gun from his latest victim.

I have all the power I need now.

Chapter 28

"Blaze him!" Dalton urged, torn by a hellacious fear strong enough to return him to his boyhood terrors...shuddering at his parents' screams, wanting his music. *Just a few songs and it will be over.*

Metallica and Volbeat and Avenged Sevenfold had gotten him through the worst nights – all the classics – and the contemporary bands, too, a little Septic Voyager and Sinkhole Pockets and even Shards for Breakfast if his parents' fights were bad enough, and Mom would eventually come in and lock the door safely behind her.

His name hadn't been Dalton Rose then. He hadn't yet carelessly chosen Dalton (the name of the home heating oil truck they'd passed on the highway at the time of his uncle's insistence that he choose a new name). He hadn't yet recoiled with shock and sharp loathing when he heard his former name called in a crowd, convinced that he'd been discovered.

"Don't go. This is a terrible idea," Dalton said, but Paul was stepping out of the car.

"It's okay. I just want to see if he needs help. You guys stay here," Paul said, but Dalton lurched out of the Mustang and walked with Paul.

Fear made Dalton feel like he was shrinking as he neared the tall man. The way he leaned against the hearse, exceedingly casual with his arms crossed, made Dalton's insides roil. It would come as no surprise if craters lurked behind the man's sunglasses.

Yet the worst part was the familiarity. Dalton was almost positive he'd seen the man before.

Leapland! Was he in the London night ride? Autobahn? No, it was the San Francisco motorcycle blaze. Definitely San Francisco. I aerial-blazed him and like seven trolleys.

"You okay, mister?" Paul said, approaching the man carefully. He reminded Paul of the Duke Ellington photos from his grandmother's collection, with his sunglasses and top hat, though this man was much taller.

"Just fine, sir. And how are you this very early morning?" The man smiled, pulling open his coat to check a golden pocket watch.

Just fine?

Dalton tapped Paul's arm. "Come on, let's go."

"What's with the hearse?" Paul questioned, unable to resist the impulse.

The man shrugged smilingly. "The job is the job, and what man ever did refuse it?" Again he consulted his watch. "Busier than usual, these last few hours. I'd say I earned my bread and jam – and a nice hot tea." He turned to Dalton. "Tea helps keep the shivers down at the latest, darkest hours."

Wondering if this man was another of evil's inventions, Paul concentrated on withdrawing slowly and without showing fear. "You stay safe, sir."

"You as well."

Paul expected an imminent wrath of bullets or lightning or both, but the man only stood there and smiled as they made their way back to the Mustang.

Almost there. Almost there.

Glancing over his shoulder one last time, Paul swelled with relief to see that the man remained at his hearse.

"Be seeing you real soon," the man said, tipping his black hat, and he finished with a name Paul had never heard.

They were back in the car, Dalton panicking. "Fuck, he said my name! He's gonna kill me!"

Dalton's face was pallid with horror, Amie stunned by his cold grip when she held him.

Paul was driving again, and they swept out and around the big man and his hearse, Amie catching sight of his wave and grin and something else, his face in flux, briefly shifting to a different form, twitching with its transmogrification. Amie wondered if she'd glimpsed less flesh than bones, less features than raw skull.

BLAZE THE GRID

Now that the hearse was reduced to a shadow in the distance, Dalton wrapped an arm around Amie and pulled her into him. She hated him for it, wishing Xeke were there, praying he was okay, but she did not push Dalton away. The night abounding with chaos, she couldn't bring herself to reject someone who, when given the choice between coming to her aid and killing the man who'd left him irreparably scarred, had chosen light over dark.

Amie traced a hand across Dalton's cheek, his scar briefly visible by the light of a house on fire.

"Did your father do this to you?"

He said nothing, leaned closer, their lips meeting for a blendered moment – and Amie felt explicitly treacherous, like she'd cut Xeke's heart out. He might have died on that wheel, the boy she'd known her whole life, the boy she loved.

She lurched away from Dalton with thoughts that the evil had brought her to this moment, meticulously arranging every detail leading up to it.

"We need to get back to the school," she said.

"Yeah, the school," Dalton repeated, looking out the window. A moment later: "They love me there, you know. I'm like the mayor."

Amie's expression iced over, not because of his words but instead the item she noticed on the seat beside her.
It hadn't been there before, but the lion mask now rested between them.

Chapter 29

The faraway wisp of moon has long since fallen beyond the hills, the colors of existence creeping back in, and still their souls have not been caged!

Raptor moves in swiftly, matching their speed, knowing where the keys are hidden. Raptor must destroy the flickering lights in the final resisters and replace them with foggy midnight.

***

After order was largely restored at the high school, the auditorium pooled with blood and piled with bodies, Steel and Virgil worked with five other men to carefully free the kid from the wheel. Even with the ladders they'd found in a storage room, the work was surprisingly challenging, the kid wrapped with more chains than a lobster boat. He was shaking and moaning, his eyes wide and gray from shock.

"Need to get him immediate treatment," Virgil said as they unwound the chains, the rest of the men holding the kid steady.

Someone had brought in stretchers, and the kid and a handful of other victims were placed on them. Walking ahead of the men carrying stretchers, Steel put down two more lunging deaders separating them from the gymnasium. But there was no help to be found inside, the makeshift hospital turned into a morgue, hundreds of victims sprawled with their throats torn open and their eyes trapped in a collective haunted stare.

Steel wished he were religious. Maybe then he could have fallen against the cushion of faith instead of falling hard on his knees. But he was empty of hope as he absorbed the enormity of death, reminded of the moment in the woods with Paul when they'd come over the rise and seen the mass grave. Revulsion and disbelief twisted up his insides like barbed wire and cut, cut, cut, cut, cut…he could feel it slicing away, even his breaths escaping in ragged bursts.

When the hand fell atop Steel's shoulder and the words came, it sounded like they were sweeping down at him from a distant ledge.

"I was at the mall that day, buying my daughter a birthday present. It was going to be the greatest surprise," Virgil said, Steel staring straight ahead as the man squatted beside him.

Together they watched as the teenager they'd saved from the wheel was put onto a cot. Amazingly, one of the doctors Steel had presumed dead stood and staggered forth, clutching his bleeding shoulder, though his concern was not for himself but his next patients. The blood flow was stanched with help from a few Freedom Riders, and the doctor moved with a little more energy, barking out directions. A dozen more Freedom Riders approached from the side doors, ready with supplies, Steel wondering if he should assist them but deciding he would only get in the way.

He kept his gun ready – that was the best assistance he could offer.

"The helplessness," Virgil continued. "That was the worst part of the whole thing. They all had weapons and masks, and you could only just stand there and watch. I should have been armed. I should have killed them all, but after the wars you just want to put the weapons away, you know?"

Virgil shook his head, his voice thinning down nearly to a whisper. "When the canisters hit the floor, I knew it wouldn't be guns doing most of the killing that day. The poison killed people in seconds. The way they just…dropped – I won't ever get it out of my head."

Virgil searched wildly about the room, then steadied again on Steel, who suddenly knew what was being recalled: the Massacre of 2020. Several cells of homegrown terrorists had targeted America's three largest cities with a newly engineered nerve agent called Nerdeg-1, killing over 700 people in a chemical attack inspired by the Tokyo terrorists who unleashed sarin on the subway system in 1995.

But Nerdeg-1 was far more powerful than sarin and similar chemicals. The terrorists had chosen malls, movie theaters, hospitals, subway and bus stations, and sporting events. The media had taken to calling it, "The Silent Massacre", for there had been no roars of gunfire, no explosions. The terrorists had been precise and efficient, shutting the victims in and gassing them before moving on to the next target. In NYC, subways had reached the next stations with dozens of deceased passengers; movie theater janitors had arrived after a screening to find the auditoriums still full, the moviegoers slumped in death. In Chicago, almost every patient and staff member in the ER of one hospital lost their lives.

"Can't believe they found me alive," Virgil said, studying the room. "I passed out, woke up in the hospital. The only thing I wanted was to call my family."

"You should get out of this place and try to find your family," Steel said. "You've done enough for everyone here."

"Not even close." He shook his head and closed his eyes to the carnage. "It'll never be enough."

***

Jazzi and Gene had come together upon arrival at the junior high school, their temporary guardians keeping close watch of them. Bea and her family, Amie's mother and grandparents, and several others did their best to keep the kids calm – but the adults' expressions betrayed gathering desperation.

Amie's father had gone back to the high school to look for her, only to return moments ago with a lost and ashen face. Amie's mom and grandparents, joined by Freedom Riders and cops, had taken the kids to the cafeteria for snacks. With his baton, one of the cops had smashed a vending machine and gotten them candy bars, but Gene wasn't hungry. He kept thinking of the man and what he'd said. He kept scanning the crowd for the face of blood and those searing eyes. They stunned you like snow down your back. They wouldn't let you look away, and once he came close and marked you with the X, you were as good as dead.

Gene had told Jazzi about the man, and she'd told him about a similar man she saw that night. She'd told him other things, too, talking about her cancer and some lady named Sena, even about how faith could get you through hard times.

Some of Jazzi's bravery had rubbed off on Gene. He was glad to have her as a friend. He couldn't find the other girl – the one with whom he'd left the second-floor classroom at the high school – but Jazzi was older and even braver than that girl. Just the sound of her voice made Gene feel less afraid.

But only a little less, for the man was out there somewhere, probably in the building, creeping and darting and flying.

Searching.

Gene looked up, saw only the ceiling. It was like coming awake from a nightmare and thinking you'd glimpsed something moving in the blackness – but when you turned on the lamp there were no threats, only the same shadows as always.

"Eat," Jazzi said, pushing a pack of M & M's across the cafeteria table, then an apple.

Gene was an only child, but he figured if he'd had an older sister she would have been like Jazzi. It would have been better with a sibling, someone to play with and talk with on the nights when Dad got mad at Mom. Dad had been yelling at Gene a lot lately, and starting to hit him when he was bad. It made Gene cry until he fell asleep (sometimes he even cried while he was asleep), but then it would all be better in the morning, Dad happy and funny and telling jokes, making Gene a big breakfast and telling him they'd go to a Sox game.

Gene smiled thinly. Maybe he could be part of Jazzi's family and Tommy's family after things went back to normal. It could be like those join-custardy deals like the other kids had, and they all seemed to like it because they got to do fun things and go to different places. They even got different rooms at different houses.

Dad and Mom would understand. Everyone had join-custardy and did family meditation.

***

Need a Coke. I could really use a fucking Coke.

Frank began to skip and hum down the high school entry drive toward Route 148, his mind ruled by music and whispering voices and a plaguing thirst.

What drives us now that the grid is gone?

Pass the bill. It will keep us safe.

Send them south, beyond the wall.

Don't kill them, not all of them. We must own their fears.

We will rule forever, but first a Coke. Need a Coke.

With two pistols Frank mercied people as he skipped and hummed "Hotel California" and "Born in the U.S.A." He fired with the joy of a kid in a squirt gun battle, loving the sounds and the sights, loving the scent of death that sang up through the mask.

The junior high! The brothers are in there. Mercy them.

"Yes, yes, but first a Coke."

Thoughts of his family occasionally broke through, but they were quickly dismissed.

Need a Coke. Need a Coke.

"I will mercy the brothers, but first a Coke."

***

When Tommy entered the junior high school cafeteria, Gene squeezed his legs and wouldn't let go, relief sweeping warmly into the boy's chest. Then Dom scooped him up, and Gene thought once more that they could all be a join-custardy family one day. They always came back for him, Tommy and Dom and Rock, and they would never leave him alone.

It would have to be join-custardy.

"It's really bad out there," Gene overheard Tommy telling someone a while later, and that made him scared. He felt like cold sheets of plastic enveloped his arms and neck, and he kept biting and picking at the skin around his fingernails.

Him. The bloody-faced man was coming soon. Gene could sense it – he could almost smell the slick iron red and the breath, hot and foul. He could feel his forehead being cut open, the wound stinging with aftershock beneath the bandage.

I will find you anywhere.

A grin had accompanied those words, the teeth gleaming, the lips loose and puffy.

For a flashing moment Gene saw the bloody face appear in the crowd, peeking down at him between two Freedom Riders. But like a nightmare monster it was gone as if it had never been there.

"It's going to be okay," came her voice, and Gene turned to find Jazzi. She was smiling softly, two bottles of water in hand. She offered him one. "Bet I can chug more than you."

Gene's fears lifted, but only for a moment.

***

Paul and Amie and Dalton repeatedly tried and failed to dispose of the lion mask, which always reappeared in the Mustang shortly after they chucked it through the windows.

They were headed south on Route 148, still several miles from the opposing Tantasqua schools. At that exact moment Frank Alexander was crossing 148 between the schools and humming "Hotel California", a steady drumbeat of gunfire reverberating in his head as he glanced down the dark road in both directions.

Need a Coke. Where's a Coke?

He started into a different hum, an old song as well, though not quite as old as "Hotel California." What was it? The elusive words almost settled for him, but they were blasted away by gunfire.

The Freedom Riders had shot at him from the bushes, but Frank had dipped and dangled and returned fire with deadly accuracy, his mind just now catching up to his body's reactions.

With casual precision he destroyed the pitiful roof snipers as well, and the way they fell into the bushes fronting the junior high school was like sweet music. Now Frank was singing something country, bellowing made-up words as he mercied one attacker after another.

"You want freedom? You got it!" Frank stood over one of them and fired until the face dissolved and the blood became the ground. "Take it! Take your freedom!"

Pulled by an even stronger instinct, Frank sprinted toward the school in a hail of mercy...and how the enemies fell, *man*, how they fell, like clattering bowling pins.

Through the front doors, into the school, countless cops and military people and Freedom Riders dropped in plumes of red mist, Frank untouchable now that he'd stolen one of their automatic rifles.

To the right. Cafeteria. The brothers are in there.

Just seconds before Frank Alexander arrived outside the cafeteria, Tommy saw the masked man in his mind. There was instant knowledge accompanying the vision, not only of what this man had done but also what he intended to do.

"Everyone get down!" Tommy screamed, lunging and tackling his brother to the floor as multiple rounds ripped through the cafeteria wall and spewed chunks of concrete. Had Tommy reacted any later, they both would have been shot in the head.

A maelstrom of gunfire ensued, Tommy and Dom scrambling beneath a table and grabbing the pistols they'd taken from the ambulance – but it was like hiding from a tornado in a tent and then pointing a gun at it.

The cafeteria doors were blown apart as if rammed by a train. A dozen soldiers and Riders were tossed aside or launched into the ceiling, the rest shredded by the masked man's gun.

Tommy, Dom, and a few others fired from beneath tables, missing, but at least they forced their attacker to retreat in a ducking zigzag to the far wall. This afforded Bea and a handful of others just enough time to whisk the screaming kids to the kitchen. One little girl remained, crouched with her hands covering her head, Bea returning from the kitchen to carry her.

Dom nearly emptied his magazine, convinced he'd hit the bastard multiple times, but still the mask angled toward them. To their left, a Freedom Rider rained automatic fire at the attacker, but the bullets might as well have been made of paper.

Why won't he fucking die?

"Get to the kitchen!" Tommy shouted, but his words were drowned. Dropping his gun, he grabbed Dom's arm and they weaved to the back of the cafeteria as the Rider's rifle was silenced.

Inside the kitchen, the kids hunkered and clung to each other. The walls shook. Trays and utensils clattered to the floor. Bea told everyone to stay quiet.

Soon the gunfire trailed off, then fell silent.

Tommy, arms wrapped around Gene, could see the man again in his mind. He was killing the remaining Riders, all of them, benefiting from the same ascendancy of evil that had been forced upon Dalton Rose. He didn't even look at his enemies as he shot them, his eyes fixed upon the kitchen door.

"He's coming for us! We have to move!"

They rushed to a side door, Tommy grabbing Bea's father's wheelchair and running to the door. Dom knew his weapon was useless, but still he pointed it into the hallway after they opened the door. Empty.

"Run! Everyone move – we're right behind you."

Dom was nauseous with fear of what they were up against. It had been overwhelming before, but this…this was checkmate. Back in the cafeteria, the slain would lie rotting for days, weeks, months, never to be honored for their sacrifices. They could have fled into the woods. They could have attempted to ride out the war in hiding, but instead they'd chosen to stay and defend the kids.

Now they were dead and nameless. Houses burned and businesses burned, society turned into tissue paper, families destroyed. Laws and badges and uniforms had provided the illusion of a fortress, but the world was in fact a cabin made of kindling.

We're all gonna die tonight.

Their head start was wasted when two kids darted into a classroom and hid in the corner.

"It's okay – you're gonna be all right. We won't leave you." Tommy reached for their hands, but that only inflamed their tears. "We have to leave the school. It's not safe here."

Back in the hallway, surrounded by adults who'd stayed to wait for Tommy, Gene tried to look past all the faces, tried to search down the hallway for the mask. He knew the man would appear any moment.

A hand in his, gently squeezing. "We'll get through this," Jazzi managed, barely able to achieve a whisper.

Dom fixed his gun down the hallway toward the cafeteria, but the man's voice arrived from the other direction.

"Gene! Gene, it's me!"

"Dad?" Gene stepped out from the group, but his father's voice had been a trick, the masked man standing fifty feet away.

"Stay back!" Dom fronted the group, joined by Tommy as he exited the classroom with the two kids.

Behind them, Rock limped in from the cafeteria, bleeding from the leg and shoulder. "Please, just let the kids go. Kill us."

"Give me my son! Gene, it's me, buddy. Come to daddy."

With both hands the man tried to tug the mask from his face, but it might as well have been glued on. He dropped his weapon and made a panicked circle as he grappled with the mask, Dom wondering if they should rush him, but no one took so much as a single step.

"See, buddy, it's me!" the man said triumphantly after ripping off the mask with an agonized moan. He squatted and held his arms out, but Gene lurched back with hot white fear, the bloody face grinning at him.

The man! He'd taken his father's face.

Frank watched with disbelief as his son sprinted away from him. Without the mask on, his head throbbed and the light stabbed needles into his eyes.

"What did you people do to my kid?" Frank grabbed up the rifle. "Did you hurt my son?"

"Drop the gun," one of the brothers said, though his order sounded more like a question.

Frank shook his head. There was an urge to put the mask on once more – he knew its powers of transformation, but with those powers came a tall price. The mask had not simply covered his face but had become his face. After a while Frank had no longer seen past the eyeholes like prison bars but *through* them like glass, and his breaths had no longer rung hollowly but freely. It had all been dreamlike and hazy, though certain parts were coming quickly back to him.

There were crying kids hidden behind the brothers, Frank resisting an urge to silence them.

"Just get away from me!" Frank warned the brothers. "Don't be like the others. I had to mercy 'em cuz they wouldn't listen. All I want is my son."

"He's not going anywhere with you." Tommy was surprised by the calm in his voice; for a moment he wondered if someone else had said it.

"You're lucky you didn't shoot your own kid back there," Dom said, desperate to pull the trigger again now that the mask was removed. "You massacred everyone else."

The man's eyes expanded darkly. "No, no, no, that's not what happened! I wouldn't just snap, are you insane? I'm a father. I've got a kid to protect. Everything I've done was to get home to Gene, everything!"

The gunshot clapped through Tommy's skull like crashing cymbals, flooring him. Toxic expectations lashed through him as he reached for his brother, but Dominick was still standing, unaffected.

Tommy didn't realize that Gene's father had been shot until Dom and Rock put additional rounds into him. The man fell onto his face, his rifle sliding away, his arms splayed, his head snapped to the side to reveal a glinting eye.

After a moment of perfect stillness and silence, they pulled the kids into an embrace, mumbling senseless words, trying to work their minds through the images that hijacked them.

No one noticed the mask, which had crept snugly over Frank Alexander's face. If not for a new vision, Tommy never would have been ready for the imminent reprisal.

"Run!" he shouted. "Everyone get out of the school!"

Chapter 30

When Xeke returned to consciousness, he was in hurried motion. The sky was blue-dark and cloud-cloaked, an evil, starless screen. The wind soldiered on, cold and whistling with the scent of smoke.

Sitting up, Xeke coughed and retched. He was on a stretcher, two men carrying him. He tried to talk but nothing came up. His memories were broken, scattered about like leaves: he'd been separated from Amie back at the facility; Virgil had brought him to the school; Dalton; the mask; the wheel.

Xeke could dimly recall what they'd done to him on the wheel. It felt like a flash from a nightmare, insignificant beyond fears for Amie and his family and his dog Zombie.

I'll find you. Tears sprang. *I'll find all of you.*

One of the men carrying the stretcher placed a hand on Xeke's shoulder. The man was familiar, his beard thick and hair long, but Xeke couldn't remember which chapter of the nightmare he'd inhabited.

Xeke began to shiver and shake. "Just rest now – close your eyes," the man said.

Behind them, unseen, dozens of other victims were being carried out of Tantasqua High School.

***

They had rescued as many survivors from the high school as they could, but the deaders had been limitless, coming from all directions – assailing in cells like thunderboomers – and there hadn't been enough people left to stop the storm.

Now there was only one last sanctuary across the street, and Steel vowed to defend these victims to the death. He prayed Paul had gotten somewhere safe, feeling useless as he did so. Paul was the man for prayers, not him, but at least he didn't feel alone this time as he glanced skyward.

"Someone up there wants us to live…I think."

But for the first time Steel worried that the rifles slung over his shoulders might run out of bullets by the time help arrived.

BLAZE THE GRID

Chapter 31

After Paul parked on Route 148 between the schools, Dalton grabbed the lion mask from the floor as they left the Mustang.

"Don't!" Amie warned. "There has to be another way."

"No, this is the only way." His eyes were dark, his voice heavy with resolve.

"You can't, Dalton! Don't let the evil in again!" Just as Paul reached to grab the mask away, the windows shattered. Behind them, the Mustang sank on deflated tires.

Having mercied a dozen more Freedom Riders, Frank was occupied by a new tune during his jog toward Route 148. "Runnin' Down a Dream." His son forgotten, the only thought as he hummed and fired was: *Need a Coke. Where can I find a Coke?*

Paul went down first, then Amie, who fell back against the car. The pain lifted to a tidal wave that didn't crest, higher and higher and higher, drowning her in seismic agony. She'd been hit in the stomach and the left leg, which throbbed in sickening, stabbing pulses, oscillating between hot-cold extremes.

"Boom, mercied your ass, nigger!" Frank was standing over Paul, who heard the wagon wheels of death riding in. He could just make out the distant whip cracks and spot two fireflies down the road that would eventually become lanterns.

Still humming, Frank dragged the girl beside the man on the sidewalk. "Interracial union?" he shouted down at them. "Nope, not allowed in this fine new institution."

Just as Frank's finger leaned into the trigger, he was rocked sideways. He landed hard on his elbow, the rifle clattering away.

Dalton scrambled back to his feet, ready to strangle the guy – except the night was suddenly replaced by the kitchen of his childhood home. It was no longer Paul and Amie on the sidewalk but Mom on the floor, bloody, shouting at him to go to his room.

And the man in the wolf mask had taken Dad's face, red with rage. Dalton could smell the alcohol, his father's eyes bloodshot.

Disoriented, Dalton seized up with fear, and for a moment all he could do was yell at the sky. "What the fuck is this? Just kill me already!"

Dad started laughing at him, a sound that cracked Dalton's lips into bloody slits. It slashed acid through his veins. It suffocated him with hate.

"I won't let you hurt her anymore!"

Dalton tackled his father, realizing after several punches that he wasn't hitting Dad but instead slicing his face into bacon strips, blood juicing away in hot spurts.

Finally able to see more clearly through his hate, Dalton beheld a massive pair of bloodstained paws clawing his father's face apart.

"You'll never hurt her again!"

Dalton bellowed thunder and triumph, then moved cautiously toward Amie and Paul.

"Jesus Lord, what in the world?" Paul came startlingly awake, pushing away the cold lips that had been poking at him.

It was the boy, Dalton, the lion mask held out in front of him.

"Xeke," Amie murmured with his touch, feeling warm and enveloped by the vestiges of sleep.

She opened her eyes to Dalton's face, pale and panicked. He brushed a hand through her hair. "It didn't work like last time. I had to mouth-to-mouth you guys."

Amie clutched her stomach and leg, the wounds vanished. Paul's injuries were gone as well. His lips moved, but he was capable only of shaking his head in disbelief.

Dalton glanced to his left. "Come on, there isn't much time! They're coming!"

Chapter 32

Steel heard the relentless march in the distance, a new wave of deaders fast approaching.

"We've got drones landing, people," he heard himself say, and a thin smile came to him with the memory. "Let's hurry! Drones landing from the south!"

The marching crashes shook the earth and cracked the pavement of the entry road, Steel expecting to turn and discover a legion of cudgel-wielding giants, their weapons barbed with railroad spikes.

The fences enclosing the football field trembled, a few sections collapsing. The water in the retention pond sloshed like a cup of soda on a turbulent flight.

To their right, the high school's parked fleet of vans and minibuses glared with headlights and lunged forward at them with screeching tires. One van bowled over a pair of Freedom Riders carrying a stretcher; two more vans narrowly missed Steel and hurtled through a fence. On the way down a short embankment, plunging and rolling, a van's Q voice informed that there were "no defects."

From the sky, debris hailed around them in a fury of wreckage, and Steel realized that drones literally were landing. Many of them were in flames.

Most of the remaining Riders dropped their stretchers and fled, leaving Steel, Virgil, and a few others to protect the victims.

"Don't do it," Steel begged the man opposite him, but the other end of the stretcher was set down.

"I'm so sorry, man, but this is just too much. I did two tours in Afghanistan, but *this* – this shit ain't natural. I think this might be the goddamn end. For real, brother."

Steel watched him rush off into the darkness, then glanced down at the teenager whose name he still didn't know. All he knew was that the kid had endured enough suffering.

"You can't have him!" he shouted at the drones. "Not unless you get me first!"

Steel tracked a burning drone coming in at a slant from the north, ticketed for him like bird shit headed for a recently washed windshield. Its glide was lifeless and yet eerily direct, a ghost ship commandeered.

Steel pulled a pistol from his collection of acquisitions and waited, not yet, not yet, a tough bastard to size up with its angled descent.

Forty feet, thirty, twenty – *Now!* – and the thing was battleshipped into pieces.

"Tanked your ass, motherfucker," he muttered, then dropped another incoming flight.

Several larger drones plummeted from directly overhead, crashing in multitudes like pennies into a fountain. The other victims on stretchers were clouted and sliced and burned, Steel giving two screaming men death by gunfire rather than flames.

"No matter what, we're going to a better place, you hear?" Steel shouted as he leaned over the teenager, and it was as if Paul were suddenly speaking through him, all of that faith talk having seemingly percolated.

The kid's panic faded and he became very still, so still that Steel thought he might have gone into shock.

"Kid, are you all–?"

Something deflected off Steel's arm, less painful than surprising. It was only an empty pizza box – Domino's, the bastards – and thankfully somebody's meatball and pepperoni had landed elsewhere.

"They're hitting us with pizza boxes, kid!" Steel laughed – a skydiving kind of laugh that challenged death. "All they've got left is pizza boxes!"

Neither of them saw Virgil in that moment. He went one against a thousand as the army approached the school from Route 148. He combated evil's inundation as he wished he'd done on the day of the massacre.

But Xeke and Steel didn't see Virgil rip through the enemy with a strength exceeding human capacity. Even as the deaders swarmed, Steel's focus remained on shooting down drones that proliferated from the sky like snowflakes.

At last the storm relented. One of the final doomed drones torched a van; another went buzzing into a bush and ignited it.

"A burning fucking bush?" Steel coughed through his laughter as he put down another drone and then two deaders. "Is that really how this is all gonna end? We couldn't have gotten anything more creative than that?"

Now Xeke was laughing as well, and soon their laughter became hysterical. Xeke didn't know why it was funny. It was just the way the guy had said it, laughter like a wall thrown up between Xeke and everything he'd lost.

Exhausted, Steel told himself to keep shooting, keep protecting. When it hurt the worst, when it felt like you were dead, that was when you were most alive. Hadn't Paul said that once? Maybe someone in the cage? Or maybe it had been a hobo in one of those boxcars headed for Chicago. Steel was too tired to remember.

"What the fuck happened to the deaders?" Steel said after dropping three more. Now there were only about fifty remaining of what had once been a juggernaut, hundreds strewn across the parking lot, Virgil staggering around and adding new corpses to the total.

"I'd ask if you needed help, but it looks like you're doing just fine!" Steel shouted across the lot.

Virgil wiped his brow and pointed toward the road. "We're just getting started."

From the south came a prolonged chorus of mechanical whines, like lawnmower blades grinding along a base of rocks. With the claps of junkyard crushers, footsteps slammed down in unison – a new army.

But there was no time for Steel to focus on this next battalion closing in on Route 148, his attention stolen by a new round of flaming projectiles. This time they weren't just drones but airplane debris: torn pieces of wings; engine machinery; landing gear. Fifty feet to Steel's right, a wheel carved out a crater in the parking lot. Down on the football field, what appeared to be the tail of a plane sheared off the scoreboard.

Even before the debris delivered its fatal blow, Steel could already see what was next. A door crept open in midair above him, a glowing white carpet unfurling for him along a staircase.

Sherman Sparks died painlessly in a storm of fresh laughter. Before taking the stairs, he dropped his guns and shed his remaining ammo. Without it he felt weightless.

"You were right, Paul, you bastard. You were right all along."

In that same span of minutes, Dalton had helped Paul and Amie into the junior high school. A Freedom Rider had seen the mask and panicked, shooting Dalton in the shoulder – but he'd been unfazed.

And that had scared Amie worse than anything tonight because she didn't know what he'd become. Had the evil been there all along, his darkness carefully manipulating her, dragging her inexorably to this moment?

Amie closed her eyes and breathed back the tears after Dalton returned her to her family and Jazzi. It suddenly came to her in bright spurts of dread that this was where they might all die. After everything they'd done to make it back to each other, what if there were no more miles left to survive? What if the school became their coffin?

Chapter 33

Frank's eyes burst open. He strained and searched and shouted, but the darkness never shallowed. He flailed with sweaty hands at the enclosing walls and pounded up at the too-close ceiling – and suddenly he knew!

He was in the psycho's casket.

"Let me out of here! I swear to God, nigger, I'll–"

Frank choked on his words and gulped them back down. He was running out of air, aware now with a flourishing panic that it was too hot in here, like a sealed car in the summertime. He wouldn't last much longer – and what few minutes he did have would shrink even further if he kept shouting.

Have to conserve. Just breathe. Just breathe.

But it was too dark and too hot to just breathe – and a barrage of memories stole his air. Hitting Gene. Cheating on his wife. Killing and killing and killing.

Mercying.

No, murdering.

But I did it to get to my son.

The memories and the claustrophobia twisted Frank's mind into a maddened thicket, the only release from which was more screaming and thrashing.

BLAZE THE GRID

At last a series of taps came against the lid, and Frank exhaled with meager relief. He wasn't buried six feet under, not yet.

This isn't happening. I'm dreaming. I shot the fucker.

Frank tried to think back, hoping that memory would provide at least a marginal clue as to where he might be. But all he could remember were those teal eyes staring down at him from behind the lion mask…and the brightest, fullest laughter he'd ever heard, like bells tolling at a goddamn church.

This isn't real. He flexed his fingers, wiggled his toes. *Wake up! Wake the fuck up!*

"Let me out of here, you bastard! My son's out there all alone – I'm all he's got left, you fucking ape!"

Frank jammed his hands so violently against the lid that he felt shearing pain in one finger and knew instantly it was broken. With a frenetic bout of sit-ups, he lifted his head and bashed it into the lid, over and over until he tasted blood.

"Let me out," he rasped. When there was no response, only a few more taps on the lid, he shouted, "You're not hurting me by doing this – you're hurting my kid! He'll die out there without me, you hear? He's got nobody left, *nobody* – I mercied his goddamn grandmother, you monkey! Try to call the cops on me, nigger! See if they come, just see if they fucking come!"

Frank was stopped by a coughing fit. Sweat poured off him; it was as if someone had locked him in a sauna and turned up the heat. Worse, he had a strange sensation of descent, elevator-like and quickening.

"What's going on? You fucking monkeys better let me out of here before I rip your eyes out!"

Suddenly Frank was silent, blessed with a miracle thought.

Frank Alexander remembered his guns.

BLAZE THE GRID

Chapter 34

Dalton was soaring high with exultation, practically scrambled. He'd brought Amie and Paul back from the brink and gotten them to safety, and no one could touch him, none of the people here and not even the creators of the masks. He'd defeated them somehow and reconfigured their powers into gifts of healing.

"Blazed your ass, dustpan," he muffled beneath the lion mask, remembering the old man who'd given him the mask.

Dalton ran out of the junior high and headed back to the high school, wondering how many more people he could help…because helping was infinitely better than hurting. It made him feel warm, lifted, like a thaw was breaking up the ice in his blood.

He'd forgotten what it felt like to view the world with anything other than hate. For years he'd wanted to hurt himself and others for his failure to protect his mother. He'd thought of suicide almost every day. He'd told that girl to piss on his face. He'd cut himself open and squeezed out the blood, though no amount of pain could fade the scars from that Christmas Eve, the guilt unremitting.

But now it was all different. He'd been shown the way somehow, a path through the darkness, and the morning sky was getting rapidly lighter.

***

"You fucking monkey, let me out of here!"

Having realized his guns were missing, Frank's only ammunition came in the form of caustic shouts.

"Let me out, you goddamn retard! You filthy animal!"

Frank felt the box lurch upward, as if lifted by a crane in a shipyard. He envisioned caskets stacked up like intermodal containers, rows upon rows upon rows, and at the center, grinning feverishly as he checked his pocket watch, was that bastard Charon.

Frank felt like he was in a furnace. The air had not only grown hotter but thicker, smokier, hardly breathable. Frank had unleashed a fury of punches against the lid upon discovering that his weapons had been seized, and what little air remained had been swiftly vacuumed up.

Now he was gasping and choking on his own carbon dioxide, drowning in the darkness, and all he could picture was Charon's grin and that godforsaken hearse.

I'm gonna die. This is it. This is really it.

Frank heaved out a shattering scream. It rebounded piercingly in the dark, and–

Suddenly it wasn't as dark. A stab of weak gray light came shafting in at the end of the casket near Frank's feet. Then another hole opened, this one in the lid directly above his face. The cool downdrafts were like swigs of water, Frank lifting his head and drinking them in. Beyond the baseball-size perforation, he could see a cobalt sky streaked with wisps of gunmetal gray.

The casket began to rock a little from side to side, gently dipping and rising.

I'm in the water! Frank realized with jagged distress. *It'll sink! I'll drown!*

The casket didn't sink, although it did begin lurching like a canoe in the open ocean. The lid groaned beneath a shifting weight, and for a moment the sky was gone, blotted out but quickly returning, then eclipsed again seconds later.

The sky came back for a brevity, but soon it was occluded again – and this time Frank could see an eye blinking down at him. When the hole widened another few inches, Frank gaped with dread, his breaths welling up, a nightmare staring down at him.

The teenager Frank had killed before stealing his scooter was now eyeing him from one side, and from the other end of the hole batted the eyes of the first man Frank had murdered. In time they were all smiling hungrily at him, the victims of his mercies forming a layered circle like spectators at the Colosseum.

Frank felt like a mouse trapped at the bottom of a trash can. He pawed up at the faces and tried to push them away, but down they came, scuttling into the casket with him, transgressing the laws of space. They moved like loose sheets in the wind, gaunt and misty, the agonies they dealt nonpareil. Frank screamed. He poked his fingers into their eyes, but they were no longer eyes but sockets, their flesh replaced by naked bones. A continuous hiss filled the casket, like sand poured down a chute, like a pit of perturbed snakes, like the Devil's beckon at the break of midnight.

Even after the suffering reached a convulsively faux apotheosis, it somehow continued to worsen, relentless and without apex…the final moments of Frank's victims felt, their suffering reciprocated in vengeful sequence.

"This is the end of the trip for you, sir. We're almost to the other side of the river now," echoed Charon's voice from some faraway place.

The casket was repeatedly jarred from beneath, as if a cluster of broomsticks were surging upward. The hissing grew louder. The casket tossed more violently.

Frank begged for his life, but a hand shot down and covered his mouth. Two more pressed against his eyes, and they were all grabbing him, holding him steady. From below, the thumping clouts pierced the base of the casket and water scalded in, the casket breaking apart.

Dozens, hundreds, thousands of corpses bubbled up from the depths. Frank could see their facial features blossom to clarity as he spun and flopped, the water turning icy, and beneath the surface countless more eyes lasered red and violet.

BLAZE THE GRID

Frank flailed in tall waves. Meteorites blazed across the sky, mountains surrounding the angry sea. Gray hands grasped and missed, Frank diving away, his head dipping beneath the surface and throbbing with frigid agony.

Gasping, feeling as though weights had been strapped to him, Frank tried to swim toward the shoreline roughly six hundred feet away, but the hands latched onto his ankles and tugged, down, down, down, his neck, lips, forehead at the surface, breaking it, choking, ice water filling his lungs, and now he was entirely submerged, gray hands like dead fish yanking him down to his doom.

Frank's final vision was that of Charon standing atop the water as if it were a sheet of glass, his arms sternly crossed. From his pocket he extracted his watch and plunked it into the sea like a coin never to glint again. A moment later a cigarette glowed orange between his lips.

***

Dalton didn't realize it was snowing until a flake settled on his face. Glancing up, he saw the precipitation drifting incredibly thinly, not even snowflakes but glazed gossamers.

Dalton's stomach went septic, for the high school ahead of him had changed. The windows and doors were different. The vehicles parked in the front lots were no longer school vans but ambulances. And the sign out front no longer read Tantasqua High School but Tri-County Community Hospital.

Fear-stricken and weightless, Dalton stopped and ripped off the mask, realizing that he'd gone too far. It was a sick feeling of miscalculation, like a pre-grid driver using the lane of oncoming traffic to pass, thinking there is enough time but then panicking and gunning it as the space closes.

And then the crash. It came one tooth at a time, Dalton not even feeling – only hearing – the first three as they clicked off the pavement. He shoved both hands against his mouth, hoping to keep the rest of his teeth from breaking free, but they were like stalactites jarred loose, their fall inevitable. More teeth dropped and his lower teeth started to swim. He tried to spit them out, but his lips wouldn't part.

"Mmmm! Mmmm! Mmmmmm!!!"

His dislodged teeth clacked and jiggled around, bobbing in a sea of blood. He fell to his knees and crawled, finally able to get his mouth open and release all but a few teeth that clung like icicles.

Pain shredded through his jaw, snow falling leisurely on him, sirens blaring in the distance. Farther down the street, houses glowed with Christmas lights.

"You thought you could change the rules," came the duster's voice, his footsteps approaching slowly, his shadow towering into view along the far sidewalk. "We've come so far with you, Rosey. You think there's time to go back and find someone else?" He shook his head reproachfully. "I didn't think you would need a reminder of what will happen if you resist. Boys, have at him."

Dozens of faces appeared from the periphery. They held Dalton down. They cranked his mouth open and clamped it, and this time the gun was shunted down his throat, curving somehow, Dalton's agony singing in his head. He tried to lift his arms, straining against their weight, but it was useless.

As consciousness was choked out of him, Dalton managed to hear a voice much deeper than the rest. Inhumanly deep. "What keeps going wrong? Why are so many of them malfunctioning?"

***

Xeke zagged and hobbled to avoid the flaming drones that ignited everything they touched, as if the earth had been drenched with gasoline. They'd all been killed, the people who'd protected him, and Xeke had crawled off the stretcher and then used a signpost to pull himself into a stand. Now he was staggering through a colossus of pain, his bones shrieking at him to stop and give up. He couldn't even straighten his knees, shambling along bent and slow but determined.

He'd convinced himself that his family had made it to the school across the street. Whether he limped or crawled or rolled himself across Route 148, he had to reach that building…but the drones were everywhere, coming from all directions. Police drones, delivery drones, media drones, surveillance drones, COMPLEX drones – they crashed by the hundreds. Xeke could barely make any forward progress after a while, too busy looking back for projectiles that glided in like frisbees, others freefalling. With the clatters of trash can lids they clapped to the pavement, and Xeke could hardly see the ones that weren't on fire, screened by the blue-black predawn sky.

Xeke made his best umbrella impression with his arms, knowing that doing so would provide limited protection from the downburst, yet still it offered a semblance of security. An even greater threat than the drones, however, was the army steadily approaching from the south. Maybe a quarter of a mile off, the marchers moved slowly with synchronized thunder-metal stomps.

After everything Xeke had suffered, he didn't even have the strength of imagination to envision the next threat. His only focus was the school and getting to his family and Amie, the rest of his mind stripped away. At times it seemed the world had been reduced to a video game of mindless reactions, and in those moments even the fear melted away and he could laugh again.

Yet each laugh was punctuated with cold, stinging tears.

***

As if the wind had suddenly changed directions and cycled new sounds through the junior high school, Amie and several others suddenly heard the next wave of attackers coming.

BLAZE THE GRID

A few cops who'd recently joined them opened the windows in the library, where most of the survivors had retreated. Many of them had escaped the massacre in the cafeteria – unsure if more gunmen had entered the school – and so they'd funneled people into the library and fortified it as best they could. It was packed to capacity, people stumbling over each other, but no one dared to separate.

The library was all they had left to defend, yet a crawling fear told Amie that it would soon fall as well. It would fall like the rest of the world.

With the library windows open, they could hear with greater clarity the massive assemblage drawing nearer on the road. It sounded like a slow-moving freight train challenged by a steep grade.

"Jesus, there must be hundreds of them, maybe thousands," Dad said. "We have to get out of here. They'll burn the school just like everything else."

Most of the others agreed, someone mentioning fish in a barrel, though a few of the cops and Freedom Riders vowed to stay and fight.

Dad gathered the family and Jazzi, bringing them into a huddle. "We'll get to the woods, stay out of sight. No more large groups – they're wiping out all the camps."

For other survivors who'd streamed into the library, like Bea's parents, the opportunity for flight wasn't feasible. Confined to his wheelchair, her father wouldn't endure if they retreated to the woods and survival became a cross-country marathon. And what about the kids they'd whisked into the library? The adults would never be able to manage them if they left the school – the kids would inevitably scatter.

Bea felt crushed and helpless. She prayed that Tommy would return, though no amount of weaponry – not even his visions – seemed strong enough to overcome the enemy.

Still, if tonight was all they had left, she wanted to be with Tommy when the world went to flames. They'd only known each other for a few hours, but amid chaos and bloodshed the hours seemed like years.

And even if they were defeated, Tommy's gift served as a constant reminder that they weren't alone.

***

Tommy, on the heels of rapidly successive visions, had sprinted with Dom across the street and behind the high school. Wrecked drones had plummeted from the sky in streaks of fire. Had Tommy and his brother run through the tier of parking lots nearest the school, they would have gone right past Sherman Sparks as he shielded Xeke Hamilton from falling debris – but instead the brothers had angled from the entry drive up to the bus circle, then around the east side of the building.

Trees were on fire, vehicles engulfed. The sky was getting lighter, but smoke preserved the dark.

BLAZE THE GRID

At last they reached the back doors. Tommy knew they would be unlocked, just as he knew the route that would take them safely up to the roof. He'd seen it all in his visions, and he'd also seen Frank Alexander killed by Dalton Rose. Bea and Gene and the others would be safe for now, though not for much longer if Tommy and Dom didn't act quickly.

They took the stairs two at a time to the roof. "You're sure you can operate this thing?" Dom was skeptical, even after the miracles he'd witnessed. His lungs burned from the sprint. He felt like he might puke, and Tommy was already advancing to the next landing – a guy who, hours earlier, had been wheelchair-bound.

Dom burst through the door to the roof behind his brother, jumping back when a drone blasted into the solar array on the west side of the roof.

Tommy rushed to the east side, where he examined the laser launcher mounted to an oversized tripod stand, his visions once again made real. Raised up over the short roof wall, the launcher could rotate to fire in any direction. Dom blinked and gaped at the weapon; twice the size of a standard rifle, its muzzle was larger than that of a bazooka.

Tommy swiveled the launcher to face south and peered through the scope. He carefully adjusted the spectrum selector. He measured out the wavelength. He accounted for the refraction range and thermal curve rate.

He did these things without even partially understanding them, his visions having supplied the instructions...and he prayed he wouldn't screw this up.

The military was forced to test these weapons in desert no-fly zones, Dom had read somewhere, for even indirectly and at great distances the lasers could cause severe retinal damage. The Russians were purportedly responsible for introducing the technology, but it suddenly seemed as though the ideas behind every weapon were in fact inspired by the true enemy.

"Put these on," Tommy said when Dom reached him, handing off a pair of goggles that brought the world to green and black. There'd only been two pairs of goggles waiting for them.

Dom eyed the weapon with fearful disbelief, the way a man might regard a device described as a time machine. "Are you sure about this? I've heard horrible shit about these things – too heavy a dose and you could open up a new Grand Canyon."

Tommy searched the road. "This is all we have left. If we don't use it, everyone dies."

In the distance, the next wave of attackers marched north on Route 148 with a thunderous boom. Tommy gazed into the scope once more, but there was no time to focus on the weapon.

The door screeched open behind them. Even if a vision had shown Tommy what would happen next, there was no way to prepare for it.

***

BLAZE THE GRID

Dalton's thoughts were senseless and fluid, slowly draining, as was his pain. He welcomed death or maybe just Leapland: a highway scene – Los Angeles? New York? – the lights extending in blurs of harsh pink and white on either side of a guardrail. Dalton was driving, threading dreamlike in and out of the gridlock, lane to lane, even using the breakdown lane, and the drivers were all grinning vacuously at him as he passed, the women with bleached hair and dark lipstick, the men with top hats and tuxedos.

Dalton felt warm breaths tickling the back of his neck, and he nearly lost the road when a sour whisper arrived: "I smell a rose, fine and sweet, and here we are, Rosey, again we meet."

Even without looking back Dalton knew it was *him*, the man who'd first brought him to Leapland. Not a man at all but a specter whose poison took many forms.

"It will all be yours," the fiend said, leaning up front and closing gray, scaly hands around Dalton's.

Even with the brake pressed, the Hellcat rocketed forward and veered into tiny pockets between vehicles. Dalton couldn't even see some of the cars they were blazing, lights reduced to blurs like scenery on the bullet train.

"All of this land – coast to coast, wall to wall – it will all be yours. When the sun rises, this corner of the earth will be yours to rule."

Dalton suddenly felt drowsy and warm, the way a few shots before bed left him.

"Why me?" Dalton murmured, fighting to keep his eyes open.

"Because you have been chosen." The voice delved down deep, illuminating memories that had been dark and frozen for years. "You have suffered." The voice whispered his real name. "You deserve this. All of this."

"Don't ever say that name again." Dalton glanced in the mirror, discovered only smoke – yet still the gray hands were closed around his own on the wheel, the grip tightening.

The smoke reminded Dalton sickly of his father's grungemaestro car show friends, the ones who used to sit in lawn chairs in front of their prized possessions on the town common every Saturday in the summer, smoking and wasting away in the heat. Dalton was forced to inhale their smoke and listen to their endless stories as he was dragged from one street rod to the next, and Jesus, were they not all the same after a while? Did they not all blend into one coarse face, one rambling story?

Dalton had pissed off his father one brutal June day with too much bitching about wanting to go home. He'd ignored Dad's warnings and subsequently found himself confined to the point of panting/sweating in the trunk while Dad had a drink at the bar. (*You embarrassed me, you little shit. You made me leave early. Next time you can walk your sorry ass home.*)

BLAZE THE GRID

Dalton had never complained at the car shows after that, knowing how hollow and useless your tears sound in the pitch black of a trunk, knowing how scary it is to wonder when you'll get out. But even at the height of terror, Dalton hadn't screamed – because if someone had found him and Dad got in trouble, that would have only meant more pain and tears.

Months later, after Dalton struck out to end a championship baseball game, his father swiped the base of the runner-up trophy across his cheek, producing a gouge whose scar would forever glare at him in mirrors. (*I came all the way here to watch that shit? You looked like you had a goddamn blindfold on up there!*) The pieces of the trophy, following a drunken stompfest outside the bar, were rained on Dalton as he cowered in the trunk, the slammed lid sending shudders through him. But that time, lying cold and shivery and quiet, Dalton heard the softest of whispers in the dark…and he felt something in there with him, flitting and crawling and brushing against him in the blackness. When Dad was finished with his drinks an hour later, Dalton emerged from the trunk shaking and incapable of speech, his hands and face smeared in blood from a dozen cuts, a damp splotch in his uniform pants and a series of thin rips in his high blue socks. Back at home, kneeling on the grass, trying not to sob and give Dad reason to send him back to the trunk, Dalton let the icy spray sting him, stripped naked and hosed off like a dog, a bottle of whiskey in his father's other hand. Long after he was clean it went on just for fun, his father laughing and drinking. (*Not a word about this to your mother, you hear?*)

Dalton hadn't lived in a big house then, and his name hadn't been Dalton Rose.

"Don't say that name," Dalton repeated, his words like an underwater language.

But how could his teeth be back in place?

Carefully, he clicked his teeth together and probed with his tongue to survey the damage. Only a few teeth were missing, a thin taste of blood in his mouth.

"I can restore you, Rosey. I can raise you up." In the mirror, a grinning face briefly emerged from the smoke: the man from Bratislava. "It's too late to turn back now. Take what is yours. Rule them."

Distantly, like a single voice at the back of a crowded room, Dalton thought he heard his mother. She was shouting at him to turn off his music, but Dalton couldn't picture her face. He could only envision the hospital curtain and what might have lurked behind it that Christmas Eve. A pair of bare white legs was visible beneath the curtain, trailing down from the bed, swinging lazily, and now the curtain was lifting, higher, higher…he could see a face – his mother's pallid face – the eyes sunken, the mouth stretched into a rictus. The neck was stitched red like baseball seams, and there was something behind her, something jittering and amorphous, not merely behind her but a part of her, its misty black tentacles extending from her sides.

"Don't let yourself suffer as I suffer," she moaned. "Choose now. Take the world."

BLAZE THE GRID

***

Dalton rushed at them, but that wasn't his real name. A new miracle was firing words at Tommy, only a few of them heard.

"Don't do this," and Tommy finished with the kid's name, Dalton staggering to a stop five feet from them.

"Your mother, she doesn't want this for you! Her voice is in my head right now – she wants you to help, not hurt."

Tommy held up both hands. He strained to hear fresh words, shouting them as soon as they were spoken in his head. "Fallen angel!" he managed just before the kid's hands reached for his throat.

Dalton stumbled backward, blinking. He carried no weapons – he was the weapon.

Dom was ready to shoot, but he knew bullets would be useless. Even the laser launcher behind them would be useless if this kid let the darkness win. The night was like a river that had gone from a trickling calm to a furious rapid, churning them relentlessly along, and now, inevitably, they were approaching a waterfall.

Dom receded a little, watching as his brother and the kid stared at each other.

"Fallen angel," Tommy repeated. "What does that mean to you?" Tommy grabbed his shoulders, searched his eyes. "What does that mean? Something to do with your mom?"

"Don't talk about her!" the kid blurted, trying to shake free, but Tommy held firm.

"You can beat this thing, Dalton! That's what she's saying – I swear to God!"

It was as though someone had clicked a mute button, for the man's lips were still moving but Dalton could no longer hear him. He could only hear *his* voice now. *I found you. I chose you. I took your pain away. I lifted you when the world wanted to take you down. You belong to me!*

Dalton felt an immense squeezing pressure at his temples. *I own your soul!*

"Just leave me alone!" Dalton pressed his hands against his head, the world reduced to a thick hissing fog. He felt a single tooth loosen and fall, then another.

Do you want the darkness again? Do you want the trunk? Do you want to rot? I will let the maggots feast on your bones. Kill the brothers! Kill them now!

The Sims brothers took Dalton by the arms, but the kid wrenched away from them, the light leaving his eyes. "You have to die, both of you."

"But your mother, she–"

BLAZE THE GRID

Dalton dove at Tommy, hands closing around his neck. Dom shot him in the head to no avail, not even fazing the kid. Depleted of ammo, Dom pounded Dalton's skull with the gun – but he might as well have been hitting a stone wall. He was helpless as the kid throttled the life from Tommy, whose face glazed over beneath the onrushing shadow of death.

But while bullets had failed, a child's scream easily penetrated the shield of darkness. As if he'd clutched a scalding pot, Dalton ripped his hands free of the man's neck. Turned. Blinked with disbelief. Stared at a screaming boy who resembled himself as a child – the boy he'd been before the cops told him Mom was dead, before he went to live with his uncle, before the Boy Scout leader told him everyone was a winner for showing up, before a man claiming to be from Bratislava took him to Leapland. Before he became Dalton Rose.

The boy's scream suppressed fear and hate, the poisons rushing out of Dalton. A momentary relief was silenced by the loosening of teeth. Dalton felt blood trickling, teeth falling, as though he'd brushed his teeth with rusted rebar beams. He tried to hold his jaw straight, but it was like attempting to save a card house from a vigorous wind.

He fell to his knees, then his stomach, blood running from his mouth. He could hear his mother's voice, but he feared he would never see her again. He would only suffer in slavery.

Suddenly Dalton couldn't breathe. Too much blood. Choking on blood.

"It's all right, Dalton – just breathe!"

The kid began to convulse, blood pouring from his lips, his eyes rolled up.
Behind them, Gene stared raptly, not at Tommy and Dom and Dalton, but instead at the black vapor gathering like smoke above them. It had come from Dalton, Gene was sure, and for a few moments it lingered. He heard a voice spill down from it, thin and windy: "He's coming for you, boy. He's coming for you all."

Just as quickly as it had appeared, the billowing mass was gone. Later, Gene wouldn't be able to remember how he'd gotten there or why he'd screamed. It all might as well have been a dream.

BLAZE THE GRID

Chapter 35

Countless survivors lost their vision that night. Anyone looking out the junior high school windows when the violet vectors raged from the laser launcher would see only blackness for their remaining years. Even the people whose exposure to the lasers was limited to indirect flashes torrenting down the halls would have significant eye damage.

Paul Shannon, who'd retreated from the library to the windowless gymnasium with several others, was bowled over by a roaring quake. Bea and her family joined other adults in covering the kids as the bleachers shook and the roof trembled and a scoreboard rattled free from the wall and crashed to the floor.

Paul was still praying for his family and Steel when the chaos relented. Steel. On one of those roads shrouded in the foglands of the past, Steel had gone from a friend to a brother. Maybe it had been on that road near the Everglades when they saw the crocodile starting toward them, or that rain-spattered road in D.C. when the next round of thunderstorms got them hurrying off the steaming pavement for cover, or that colorful portrait of a road through the Rockies.

Paul eyed the doors, wondering if Steel's road had reached its end. Though Paul's vision was restored, he needed his guide more than ever.

When their group exited the school many minutes later and hazarded down the entry drive toward

Route 148, they benefited from just enough distant firelight to save themselves. Had it been full dark, they would have walked off a cliff and fallen into a dust-steamed abyss where the road should have been.

***

Having risked leaving the school earlier, Amie and her family plodded through the cold, damp woods. The thunderous sounds of the marching army had diminished with distance, but now they were gone altogether.

Glancing back toward the road a few moments ago, Jazzi and Grammy had both seen a purple flash dagger through the trees, Jazzi describing it as too bright for lightning. They'd all heard the sky-splitting thunderclaps that had followed it.

"The lights hurt my eyes," Jazzi said, rubbing them.

"Me too. I'm still seeing spots," Grammy added.

"Was it a bolt, or a burst of light?" Dad said.

"A burst," Jazzi answered, stretching both arms out wide. "It lit up the whole forest."

"A bomb?" Grammy wondered.

"Come on, we should keep moving," Grandpa urged. "Gotta beat the sun and find somewhere to hide."

"He's right," Dad said. "Even the woods won't be safe for long. We have to find a hidden shelter – maybe an abandoned building somewhere."

"They're burning all the buildings," Grandpa said. "We're better off hiding in the woods."

Dad shook his head. "We'll be fine. The feds will eventually get this under control – we just have to wait it out."

Spoken without conviction, his words held no definition. His expression, however, was bright with the terror he hoped to hide.

They walked a mile farther, guided by the strengthening predawn light. Birds forewent their morning songs. The air was smoky and haunted, their breaths expelled in tired puffs. It seemed to Amie like the trees would continue interminably, yielding neither to a road nor a clearing. It seemed like the sun would remain at its precise angle for eternity, providing no hope for recovery.

But a short while later they arrived at both a clearing and a road. Parked at the far edge of that thin road was a hearse – the same hearse from before, Amie quickly realized. And leaning against the hearse, hands in pockets, was the man with the suit and sunglasses.

Dad and Grandpa were quick with their weapons. They'd acquired pistols dead men would no longer need at the junior high school – and a few knives as well.

"Hands up! No quick movements!" Dad ordered. They were less than one hundred feet from the man and closing.

"Get your goddamn hands up!" Grandpa shouted, a two-handed grip failing to keep the shakes away. "I won't tell you again!"

But the man ignored their warnings and lit a cigarette, Amie noticing an open casket extending from the back of the hearse.

"I have one final charge before daybreak, I'm afraid," the big man said, eyeing Jazzi. "The girl is to come with me."

"No!" Amie stood in front of Jazzi. "Take me instead!"

"But it isn't your time," the man said, adjusting his sunglasses and checking his watch. "I don't make the decisions – I'm but a courier, a ferryman of every river, a driver of every…well now, would you look at the time!" Grinning, he pointed to the east as the first coin edge of sun peeked through the trees. "At last the night is over, but its darkness will remain. A long, winding road lays ahead, and very few will see its end."

From his pocket he extracted a small notebook and made a series of slashes and remarks, writing with the speed of a doctor scribbling prescriptions. Looking up again, nodding at Jazzi, he said, "Now that the day is new, last night's charges have expired. May you all be safe upon the road."

BLAZE THE GRID

None of them said a word as he tipped his hat and returned to the hearse. Glancing back where the casket had been, Amie couldn't find it. The hearse's doors were shut now and the vehicle started forward like a wraith on wheels, making not a sound.

They didn't speak or even move until the tail lights disappeared into a smoke-patched stretch of road. The sun, meanwhile, was coming up fast. For Amie, it was like waking from a nightmare and wondering if the demons had not been limited to her mind but had instead stalked up to her bedside, their leering faces just inches away when she woke.

Chapter 36

Since returning to the junior high school, the Sims brothers had gone without food and rest. They'd assisted dozens of victims who'd been blinded by the laser, trying to combat their agony with small comforts, finding mostly futility in every room.

Finally dawn arrived. Stretched out achily on a classroom floor, Gene and Bea beside him, Tommy listened to the sobbing and moaning of those whose vision he'd destroyed. Many of them had required restraint so they wouldn't hurt themselves or others. A handful had killed themselves with guns in their possession at the time of the laser launch. Bea had tried to keep them nourished with the remaining food from the cafeteria, but nothing could quell their panic.

The launcher had obliterated thousands of enemies, but not without devastating consequences. Closing his eyes, Tommy replayed the decisive moment over and over. Vividly, he could see the fissure widening to a dark canyon, countless enemies tumbling into the blackness. It had been like switching a hose to the jet setting and spraying relentlessly at a sand castle until it broke apart.

It had to be done. They would have killed us all.

There were only two doctors presently in the junior high school, but both of them had been blinded. The supply of equipment and medications had been destroyed at the high school. A nurse, a cop, a paramedic, and several Freedom Riders had left the

BLAZE THE GRID

junior high seeing shapes and shadows following the laser flashpoint.

There was nothing more to be done to help the wounded, except–

Dom crossed the classroom and went to the windows, where a blinded elderly woman in a chair heard his footsteps and begged him to kill her.

Dom gently squeezed her hand. Her eyes were bandaged, her lips quivering. Her face was gray with agony.

"Please end it. End my suffering," she rasped. "My eyes are burning. I can't bear another minute."

"We're gonna find help for you – all of you. Just hang on a little longer."

Dom didn't know what else to say so he said nothing, turning away from the old woman to face the window. He stared out past the oak trees winding along the entry drive and the bus circle, where just yesterday kids had been dropped off and picked up. Farther out, in the middle of Route 148, a pair of headlights slowly approached from the south.

Impossible. Despite the canyon, the headlights gradually expanded and crossed the area of sundered earth without incident.

Dom felt cold and slippery with panic, the way one might feel upon waking at midnight and discovering a strange vehicle parked in the driveway.

"It's not over," Dom muttered. "It's only just beginning."

BLAZE THE GRID

Chapter 37

As the sun climbed the chain lift toward its afternoon peak, dozens of Freedom Riders started their engines with a collective roar and thundered north into Brookfield. They'd wanted to head south on Route 148, but that would have required a bridge over the newly formed canyon.

Many of the Riders had fought decades earlier in Afghanistan or Iraq, never imagining that the scars of war would be reopened at home. But now their own neighborhoods were torn by war, house after house burnt down to cinders and soil, survivors limping back to their homes and searching for signs of hope amidst the rubble.

A faceless enemy had destroyed their country, not merely hitting their homes but their hearts, tearing at every thread of freedom. In only a night the nation had been razed – and what was the enemy's next move?

Xeke finally reached his neighborhood just before sunset, limping down streets made foreign by a veil of smoke, stopping often to glance behind him. No one there but him and the road. The sky was hazy and angry and distant beyond jagged clouds. The air was cold and toxic, sour with death and misery. It was the stench of war, Xeke thought, hobbling along, bloody and broken.

The wind was dying off, and each time a branch scraped or groaned Xeke would stop and fan his pistol's glare across an ocean of shadows. They'd armed him before he left the junior high school, but the weapons now seemed pointless. There were only so many rounds…and too many enemies.

Xeke wondered if his family would be waiting for him at home. He wondered if anything was left of his home; perhaps only memories awaited him.

They're alive. I just have to get home. They'll all be there.

Despite witnessing one burnt-out house after another, Xeke was nonetheless brought to his knees by the sight of his own home black with ruin. Smoke whispered through the wreckage, the house having collapsed but for the north-facing wall, its smashed windows like the eyes of a suffering animal.

Distantly, gunshots shredded through the evening cold.

Xeke searched the remains of his home until his hands were black and darkness began to swallow the neighborhood. The smoke made him cough and abraded his throat raw, but still he shouted for his parents and his dog. Only the distant gunfire responded.

Afraid he might not be able to get back up if he lied flat, he sat with his back against the mailbox. A night breeze soughed through the twisted heap that had been his home, Xeke wondering where to go now that nothing was left. He clutched his head with both hands, tried to drive out the vertigo that had tormented him since being rescued from the wheel. Even now, sitting still, he felt like he was spinning.

Darkness settled coldly over the neighborhood, hiding the smoke but not the stench. The patches of gunfire became more frequent in the night. Minutes passed, Xeke scared to fall asleep but helpless to resist it. When he awoke, he spun around and pointed his pistol. He'd heard someone in the brush between his yard and Mr. Korach's burnt-up property.

Xeke's gaze drew in from Korach's yard to the dark brush, where someone was creeping closer…but a beloved jingle expelled all fear. Xeke set down the pistol and used the mailbox to pull himself up through the pain, barely getting his legs beneath him before Zombie leaped into his arms.

When he finally regained enough energy to move again, Xeke and Zombie started down the night road, a pair of survivors wandering a desolate furnace of a neighborhood. Amie had once lived toward the end of the street, in a house that was now burnt and totaled like all the others, but maybe her current house had been spared.

It was a short drive to Amie's house, but in Xeke's condition he would probably have to walk until midnight to get there.

"Come on, Zombo, let's find some water." The dog whined as if expressing approval.

Upon first sight of distant headlights, Xeke again pulled the pistol from his belt and started toward the woods – but then he heard a familiar rumbling blast. Amie's grandfather! With its broken exhaust manifold bolt, the pickup truck sounded like an eighteen-wheeler. Xeke and Amie had gone out beneath the stars in her grandfather's hayfields a few times in that old rig, enough for him to recognize the truck when it came into view.

"Oh my God, it's him!"

Amie couldn't believe it. They'd gone by Xeke's house that afternoon and waited for a few hours, glancing back and forth down the road and occasionally up at the mountain of debris that had been a house, *his* house. It was as if a line of tornadoes had bulldozed across the state, demolishing anything in their paths. Finally, with a long hug that afternoon, Dad had told Amie she needed to prepare for the worst. Thousands had died, and they'd only seen a few hundred survivors all day.

"We're the lucky ones," he'd said. "We're very blessed to all be together."

That morning, a Freedom Rider had stopped his SUV for them and dropped them off at Amie's grandparents' remote farmhouse in Monson, which hadn't been discovered by the enemy. The Freedom Rider had been invited to stay at Grandpa's farm – one kindness exchanged for another while others exchanged gunfire – but the man had ventured back out to find his wife and grandchildren.

That evening, at Amie's request, her father had driven her in Grandpa Joe's old truck – of all his vehicles, it had the most fuel – back to Xeke's neighborhood for one final search. They'd almost given up and gone home after darkness fell, but Jazzi had asked if they could search for a few more minutes. Having insisted on joining them to search for Xeke, the girl had said she had a good feeling, her eyes wide with hope in spite of all she'd seen and suffered.

Within five minutes of Jazzi's request, Dad had alerted them that someone was walking up ahead. Amie had initially thought the guy was too tall, but then, a little closer, she'd known.

Amie leaped out of the truck, pain springing through her knees. Xeke's lips were icy, his cheeks bandaged, and there was very little strength in his embrace. His dog jumped and howled and made a jubilant circle around them.

Dad helped Xeke toward the truck. "Your family. Does anyone know where they could be?"

Xeke's headshake scarcely qualified as movement. Amie hugged him again, fearing that he wouldn't go with them.

"Did you walk all the way here?" Gun ready, Dad made frequent searches of the road, the neighborhood dark beyond their headlights.

"Everything's destroyed," Xeke said. "People are still getting killed. I've heard the gunshots all night."

Watching Xeke, who traveled only with his dog, Amie was suddenly aware that she and her family were indeed the lucky ones. They were all together. They had a house, food, water, transport, medicine. They had the company of a small girl whose determination rose higher than mountains. Jazzi had been fighting an uphill battle even before the chaos reigned, and yet still she smiled. Still she remained hopeful. And if Jazzi could find cause for hope, then hope was an obligation for the rest of them.

Amie took Xeke's hands. "We're staying at my grandparents' house in Monson. It wasn't burned – none of the houses on his street were burned. You should come with us. You need to rest – we'll look for your family again tomorrow, I promise."

Xeke nodded, Dad helping him and Zombie into the bed of the truck. Amie and Jazzi climbed into the bed of hay as well, Zombie licking Jazzi's face.

"Stay down and out of sight. Everyone with a vehicle is a target," Dad warned before sliding into the driver's seat. "If someone shoots us and we crash, you run. You don't wait for me – you run."

Lying beside each other in the truck, looking skyward, Xeke and Amie found themselves in the same position as last night.

Back to where it all began, she thought, squeezing his hand.

The truck growled into motion. Gunshots echoed through the night, but they were relegated to dark, distant roads and battles unseen. Dad avoided populous sections on their way back to Monson, zigzagging through a series of backroads to minimize their exposure.

It was 2030 in the United States of America, a nation in tatters. There were no laws, no authority of government or science or reason, everything defied and destroyed. The outrageous was to be expected, the impossible made real by a thousand horrors.

"I told you we'd find Xeke," Jazzi said, turning to Amie.

Amie pulled the girl against her. Just as she began to pray, a shooting star broke across the sky, knifing impeccably through screens of smoke.

"We're together – all of us," Amie said. "That's all that matters."

Chapter 38

When Dalton came groggily and achingly awake, he might as well have been a boy again. He was confined in darkness, panting and scared, remembering his father's trunk and how, desperate for escape, he'd hit his head on the lid that sweltering June day after the car show. It had been Sixties Day and Best in Show, Dalton somehow recalled, and Dad had been mad at him again...*You made me miss the awards, you little puke. Why do I even bring you? Can anything ever be easy with you?* When his father had finally opened the lid and released him, there'd been alcohol on his breath and hatred in his eyes. They'd been in the dusty parking lot behind the bar, a freight train rumbling past, two ladies jogging in brightly colored outfits up on the bridge, the world spinning on as the boy suffered.

His name was Dalton Rose now, and this time no one was around when the trunk lid came slowly open. Only the cold, smoky dark greeted Dalton as he pulled himself into a sitting position. The wind whispered in his ears. Branches creaked but did not sway. A wisp of faraway moon dipped toward the horizon; otherwise the sky was bitingly black.

Pain lashing at his knees and hips and mouth, Dalton hopped down from the trunk and stumbled into a circular clearing, gasping when he realized the car was his father's old GTX – the one that had first imprisoned him in its trunk. To his right, the road curved off into the woods, portaled darkly by tall trees, no other vehicles in sight.

BLAZE THE GRID

Moments later Dalton heard rustling and snapped twigs in the woods. Unhurriedly, dozens of men emerged, grinning and leering, each in possession of a torch or lantern. The old man who'd given Dalton the mask was foremost among them, his grin the widest.

"You failed us, Rosey. You're of no use to us anymore."

Some of the men carried knives, others saws and pitchforks. Four men hefted a wooden cross, the hunger in their eyes like that of wild dogs.

"You wanted to be chained up, didn't you, Rosey? You wanted the pain," the dustlord glared. "You should have listened, you little defect, though I suppose we shouldn't have expected too much from you. Countless beatings and you never figured out that it wasn't the alcohol that made Daddy hate you. It was the sight of your defect bastard face reminding him of Mommy's betrayal."

Dalton tried a hobbling escape, but the men encircled him with weapons pointed, dozens more coming from the smoke-swirled woods.

"Still, even a *defect* could have been the chosen one – but now you're nothing!" Dusty shouted.

Two of them lunged at Dalton. Despite the shredding pain, he shoved down the first man and dodged the other's knife. He kicked another guy but lost his balance, his foot sliding on the moist grass, sending him into a sprawl on his back.

The attackers' faces blotted out the sky, edging closer, closer, grinning, laughing, a tower of smoke rising all around them.

"Nail him to the cross!"

"Let the ravens have him!"

"Leave his body for the maggots!"

Large shadows flared up in the smoke, winged creatures taking flight from their shoulders.

Dalton was paralyzed by a grip around his ankle, burning acidly, whispers hot in his ears. The smoke thickened. Wings overspread the darkness.

Just as a string of chains was wrapped around Dalton's ankle, his attackers turned collectively toward the road, their eyes flashing in the torchlights like skittish deer.

"He's coming," Dusty snarled. "Damn him. What is he doing in this realm?"

Capable of spasmodic movement, Dalton dragged himself toward the road as his attackers fled into the woods. Moments later, having freed himself from the chains, Dalton saw headlights bobbing distantly, breaking through the trees. Barely making a sound, the hearse pulled up and the driver stepped out, his shoes whispering leisurely along the pavement.

Dalton staggered to his feet and nearly fell. He remembered being drunk for the first time. He remembered trying to protect his mother and getting punched for the first time. He remembered Mom hugging him one night after Dad hit them both. She ran her hands through his hair and said she loved him, that she would make it up to him, that Dad was only mad because of work.

Dalton remembered his first trip to Leapland. He remembered blazing the grid with Amie and how surprised he'd been to find happiness with her on the road.

But it hadn't lasted. It never lasted.

Dalton knew who was approaching even before the driver lit a cigarette and exhaled smoke and shadows. But in spite of what Dalton had felt before, this man offered nothing to fear; Dalton knew this infallibly now.

"I said we'd be seeing each other real soon," the man chuckled as he consulted his watch.

The sky was fast with scudding clouds, the smoke scuttling away in ropes and vines, tugged back into the forest by shadow hands.

"Am I dead?" Dalton murmured, wondering at the sudden absence of pain.

"You are very much alive and purposeful." The man stamped out his cigarette. "Come now, for the night is short and I have many stops to make. Let us drive for a while, and then the road is yours."

The hearse was hot and smoky. Dalton knew it was beyond coincidence that "Don't Fear The Reaper" crackled over the radio when he slid into the passenger seat. The dashboard flickered orange, though the usual array of instrumentation was missing, replaced by a series of arrows.

Gloved hands clenching the steering wheel, the man glanced over at Dalton and offered a cigarette. Dalton accepted, smiling as the radio rattled on about the Reaper. He inhaled the smoke and let it pour out, savoring the absence of pain, savoring the full complement of teeth currently in place.

"What next?" Dalton said after a while, wondering if it was all just a Leapland coder. The architects were constantly improving the duration and vividness and biometry of the product, to the extent that one of Dalton's latest leaps – Naked Salem – had transported him to a Halloween ripper packed with masks and costumes and sex. He'd shoved through dozens of partyers in search of his clothes, unable to find a single article, instead putting on some guy's cocaine-dusted vampire costume and hurrying out of the house. The keys to the Maserati were left in the ignition, and a bearded hobo was sleeping in the back seat with a spilled beer on his gut. It wasn't until midnight – four hours after Dalton had taken the coder – that Leapland had finally faded to reveal his half-dressed image in the bedroom mirror, a puddle of vomit smeared into the carpet, his shoulder hurting, his eyes bloodshot, a fire and ice condom filled on the bed. You were supposed to bungee yourself in place before going to Leapland, but Dalton had always preferred freefall leaps. Half the fun was you never knew where you'd be bleeding after you reentered the atmosphere.

BLAZE THE GRID

The driver watched Dalton, not the road, his hands reacting on their own. "Everything you've seen tonight must seem like Hell on Earth, but unfortunately it's only the antechamber to Hell. Unimaginable horrors are destined for these roads, and you must be prepared for them."

"Me? What the fuck am I supposed to do?"

"Heal the wounded, bring people together – just as you've done tonight. But your gift doesn't originate from a mask or the darkness within. It comes from the light."

"They'll destroy me."

"They intend to."

"They were gonna nail me to a fucking cross! They keep knocking my teeth out every two minutes."

"Which is why you must be prepared. They know your power, and they'll spare no resource in attempting to eradicate you and the others."

"The others?"

"Just watch for a moment." The man turned back toward the road and clicked off the headlights, the hearse plunged into blackness.

"What the fuck are you doing, guy?"

When the headlights returned, they were on a new road – a gravel track bordered by barren moonlit lands, not a tree in sight. A sign in the distance read:

DALTON HIGHWAY NORTH
DEADHORSE, AK – 50 MI.

"A lonely road, indeed," the man commented. "The James W. Dalton Highway. It shares your name – your current name, that is."

"Who are you?"

"A man who's broken an awful lot of rules tonight. A few folks recently knew me as Mr. Charon, but my name isn't important. All that matters are the directions I convey."

Headlights off. Over a minute later they returned to reveal Times Square in flames.

Off, on. Swamplands.

Off, on. A massive sign for a motel. Behind it a sign for Historic Route 66 Museum.

"Kingman, Arizona," the driver said. "Last I was here, there was no time for me to see the sights. A boy got drunk on prom night and crashed into a tree. Two hours later an old woman had a heart attack and rolled her van. Same road – three miles apart."

Off, on. A highway inferno. A sign for the Basketball Hall of Fame.

The driver tossed his cigarette out the window and lit another. "So many destinations, so little time. A lot of people are depending on you, son."

BLAZE THE GRID

Dalton recoiled when the man proceeded to say his name. He'd said it before, but this time Dalton felt no threats from Charon, only fear of what would come next.

Headlights off, on. This time Charon parked the hearse on a road surrounded by woods engulfed in flames.

For the next five minutes Charon spoke and Dalton listened with mounting terror.

"…You'll have to walk the rest of the way. The road will provide directions that words cannot. Hurry now, and don't forget the instructions I've given you."

"I can't do this. I'm nothing – I couldn't even save my own…"

His words wouldn't finish, replaced by tears.

"You can do this. Your life has been hard, but it has made you ready. Do you think you were chosen at random?"

Dalton put both hands behind his head and struggled for a clean breath. For a while his thoughts were clouded, but a sudden and piercing determination knifed through the fear. It dried his tears and cleared his mind.

"The monster has tormented you all these years, always at your back, darkening every day," Charon said, lighting another cigarette. "You think your past makes you weak, but nothing could be further from the truth. Every obstacle on our roads makes us who we are. They prepare us for the road ahead." He sighed out tendrils of smoke. "You're ready for the tallest order yet, son. Time favors you, and the road beckons."

BLAZE THE GRID

Thanks, friends, for your continued support of the *Gridlocked* series. The next book in the series, *The Grid Awakens*, will transport you down increasingly terrifying roads haunted by old foes and new fiends.

MEET THE AUTHOR

A lifelong resident of Massachusetts, Kevin Flanders has written over ten novels and multiple short stories. In 2010, he graduated from Franklin Pierce University with a degree in mass communications, then served as a reporter for several newspapers.

When he isn't writing, Flanders enjoys spending time with his family, playing ice hockey, and traveling to a new baseball stadium with his father each summer. He also takes part in several functions and mentors student writers.

But no matter where Flanders travels or who he meets along the way, he is always searching for inspiration for the next project.

The author resides in Monson, MA.

For more information about upcoming works, visit www.kmflanders.wordpress.com.

Made in the USA
Middletown, DE
26 June 2022